Praise for the First Daisy Thorne Mystery

DEATH AT A C

"Sharper than a pair manicure, Daisy Thorne is no ordinary hairdresser and when her best friend's mother is murdered, she combs through clues looking for the killer. *Death at a Country Mansion* has more twists than a French braid."
—**Sherry Harris**, author of the Sarah Winston Garage Sale mysteries and the Chloe Jackson Sea Glass Saloon mysteries

"*Death at a Country Mansion* is a fun romp through the British countryside, with Daisy Thorne, hairdresser, leading a colorful cast of characters to solve the murder of her dear friend Floria's famous mother. Daisy is smart, savvy, and full of spirit. This book has a delightful puzzle with a satisfying ending. Everyone who loves a manor house mystery will love this one."
—**Nancy Coco**, author of the Candy-Coated mystery series

"Multiple suspects, myriad motives, and a missing Modigliani add up to murder at the manor. Louise Rose Innes is constantly twisting the story just as we, the reader, believe we've figured out the murderer. If you enjoy British manor houses, a touch of budding romance, and a good mystery (like I do), I highly recommend *Death at a Country Mansion*."
—**Vikki Walton**, best-selling author of the Backyard Farming mystery series and the Taylor Texas mystery series.

"*Death at a Country Mansion* is a wonderfully twisty murder mystery that will keep the reader guessing while also bringing delight. I loved the characters, especially the employees of our sleuth's hair salon, and the cooperation between sleuth and police is a refreshing change to the typical cozy tension there. Throw in a little romance, a little art history, and a gorgeous mansion, and you have a page-turner that is fun and intriguing."
—**ACF Bookens**, author of the St. Marin's Cozy mystery series

"*Death at a Country Mansion* is a wonderful debut by Louise R. Innes. The book opens at a stately mansion, Brompton Court, in a charming town in Surrey, where a famous singer is found dead at the bottom of the grand staircase. Our inquisitive sleuth and hair salon owner, Daisy Thorne, helps a handsome detective solve the murder. With an endearing cast of characters, including Daisy's good friend, Floria, this tightly plotted mystery will keep you guessing until the very end!"
—**Tina Kashian**, author of the Kebab Kitchen mystery series

Books by Louise R. Innes

Romantic Suspense
Going Rogue
Rogue Justice
Loveable Rogue
Wild Rogue
Rogue Agent
A Passion So Wild
Personal Assistance

Romantic Thriller
Undercurrent

Contemporary Romance
Perfect Friends
Holiday Fling
2nd Time Around
Forever Yours
Falling for the Greek Billionaire
Antarctic Affair
The Italian Inheritance

Romantic Novellas
The New Year Resolution
The Love Formula

Death at the Salon

A Daisy Thorne Mystery

LOUISE R. INNES

KENSINGTON
PUBLISHING CORP.

www.kensingtonbooks.com

KENSINGTON BOOKS are published by

Kensington Publishing Corp.
119 West 40th Street
New York, NY 10018

Copyright © 2021 by Louise R. Innes

All rights reserved. No part of this book may be reproduced in any form or by any means without the prior written consent of the Publisher, excepting brief quotes used in reviews.

To the extent that the image or images on the cover of this book depict a person or persons, such person or persons are merely models, and are not intended to portray any character or characters featured in the book.

This book is a work of fiction. Names, characters, places, and incidents either are products of the author's imagination or are used fictitiously. Any resemblance to actual events or locales or persons living or dead is entirely coincidental.

If you purchased this book without a cover you should be aware that this book is stolen property. It was reported as "unsold and destroyed" to the Publisher and neither the Author nor the Publisher has received any payment for this "stripped book."

All Kensington titles, imprints, and distributed lines are available at special quantity discounts for bulk purchases for sales promotion, premiums, fund-raising, educational, or institutional use.

Special book excerpts or customized printings can also be created to fit specific needs. For details, write or phone the office of the Kensington Sales Manager: Attn.: Sales Department. Kensington Publishing Corp., 119 West 40th Street, New York, NY 10018. Phone: 1-800-221-2647.

The K logo is a trademark of Kensington Publishing Corp.

First Printing: April 2021
ISBN-13: 978-1-4967-2982-8
ISBN-10: 1-4967-2982-X

ISBN-13: 978-1-4967-2983-5 (ebook)
ISBN-10: 1-4967-2983-8 (ebook)

10 9 8 7 6 5 4 3 2 1

Printed in the United States of America

For Sheila Renn

Chapter One

The tiny brass bell attached to the front door of Ooh La La hair salon tinkled as Liz Roberts, head of the Edgemead Women's Institute, marched in, bringing with her a blast of rain-drenched wind.

"Heavens, it's appalling out there," she said as she shook out her umbrella and left it dripping against the antique hat stand. "I trod in a puddle outside the Fox and Hound, and I swear I've ruined my new suede boots." She glanced disdainfully down at her feet.

"Can I take your coat?" Daisy smiled sympathetically.

Liz removed her practical Barbour raincoat and handed it over. "Thanks, Daisy dear. Oh, it is nice and warm in here. Hopefully, my shoes will dry out."

"Come on, we're over here." Daisy led her to one of the comfy leather chairs positioned in front of a gilt-framed mirror. "Would you like a cup of tea?"

"You wouldn't happen to have anything stronger, would you?" Liz arched an eyebrow. "I've had such a trying day."

Daisy hid her surprise. Liz seldom indulged. "Of course, you know me. I've always got a bottle of something in the back." She turned to Penny, who was sweeping up the hair from her last client. "Could you pour Liz a glass of the sav blanc?"

Liz picked up the latest edition of *Vogue* magazine and flicked through it without looking at any of the pages. "Thanks for fitting me in this late. I hope I'm not putting you out."

Daisy picked up her comb. The table containing the tint, foil wraps, and various utensils had been prepared in advance. Liz was having her usual mixture of highlights and lowlights. "We close at nine on a Saturday, so you're our last customer of the day." It wasn't like she had anything better to do, anyway, and the weather was so dire that the sofa, a takeaway pizza, and a box set was calling her name.

Penny returned with a glass of wine and handed it to Liz.

"Thank you, dear."

Daisy noticed her hand was shaking. "Are you alright, Liz?"

The formidable face showed just a hint of vulnerability. "Yes, of course, dear. It's just the speaker for this Thursday's meeting cancelled at the last minute, leaving us in the lurch. She's pregnant." She rolled her eyes at Daisy. "Pregnant women are always so unreliable."

Liz Roberts wasn't known for her tact.

"What was she going to talk about?" Daisy asked.

"We were going to make Christmas wreaths." Her mouth turned down at the corners. "I have no idea what to do now. I suppose I'll have to ask Mrs. Radisson to give us her rosemary turkey stuffing demonstration again."

Daisy parted Liz's hair into segments and began to apply the tint. "I have a friend who makes her own Christmas cards. They're really lovely with sparkles and little bows on them. If you want, I could ask her if she'd be prepared to do a workshop for you?"

Liz's face lit up. "Oh, Daisy, would you? That would be fantastic. I really am at a loose end."

Daisy nodded. "No problem. I'll call her tonight."

Penny reappeared from the back wearing her coat and scarf. "Right, I'm off, Daisy. Thanks for letting me go early. I'll lock up next Saturday, I promise."

"That's okay. Have fun tonight at the hen party."

Penny glanced at her wristwatch. "I won't get there much before nine because I'm going home to change first. I'm meeting Niall later." Her eyes sparkled. Niall was Penny's new beau, and while Daisy didn't altogether approve of the match, she had to admit Penny seemed happy. Unfortunately, knowing Niall, the relationship was unlikely to last. Still, stranger things had happened.

"I'm sure the party will be going on for a while," said Daisy. "Those girls were gearing up for a big night." All three of Penny's model friends had been in earlier to get their hair done for tonight's celebrations. They'd brought a bottle of bubbly with them and were giggling merrily by the time they left.

Penny grinned. "Yes, they were. I'll see you on Monday. Bye."

After she left, Liz glanced up at Daisy. "That man is double her age. He ought to be ashamed of himself."

Daisy shrugged. Niall was a notorious womaniser and an ex-husband of the late Dame Serena Levanté, the infamous opera diva who'd been murdered last year in her country mansion. It was Daisy who'd helped crack the case. "He is very handsome," she allowed.

Liz frowned. "If one goes in for that sort of thing. I'm more inclined to think it's his money she's after."

Daisy shook her head. "No, not Penny, she's not a gold digger." She wrapped a strip of foil around the highlight and squeezed it closed. "You have to admit, Niall does have something of the Heathcliff about him. I can picture him riding bareback through the moors on one of his prized racehorses, can't you?"

Liz gave her a sharp look. "Don't tell me you're smitten too?"

Daisy laughed. "You know me better than that, Liz. All I'm saying is I can see the appeal."

Liz grunted.

Once the foils were done, Daisy placed Liz under the dryer and took the messy utensils and dishes into the kitchenette to wash up. BBC Radio 3 was playing *La Calisto*, Cavalli's opera of pursuit and transformation, and the dramatic music filled the salon. With a contented sigh, Daisy washed up and then poured herself a much-needed glass of wine. The back door was banging in the wind, so she wedged a piece of paper towel in the crack. Exactly ten minutes later, she switched off the dryer.

"Come over to the basin," she told Liz, and proceeded to wash and condition her newly dyed hair.

"Do you want a trim?" Daisy asked, once Liz was back in the chair in front of the mirror, admiring her new colour.

"Yes, just half an inch off the bottom."

Daisy reached into the drawer for her scissors, but they weren't there. How strange. She always put them back in the top drawer of her workstation—in fact, she was fastidious about it. Her eyes roamed over the countertops, but they weren't there, either. Frowning, she opened Penny's drawer and used hers. Each stylist had their own scissors to avoid confusion.

"How are things going with that hunky detective of yours, Daisy?" asked Liz, causing Daisy's head to pop up.

"I don't know what you mean," said Daisy, avoiding eye contact.

"I thought you two were a thing." Liz arched an over-plucked eyebrow.

Daisy took a gulp of her wine. "Oh, no. We worked together on the case last year, but that was it. There's nothing going on between us."

"If you say so, dear." Liz winked at her.

Daisy sighed. She hadn't seen Paul in months. He was situated in Guildford, which was a good forty-minute drive from Edgemead. He'd taken her out once after the Serena Levanté case, but then Daisy had gone away with her friend, Floria, to the south of France in the summer and they'd lost touch after that. According to Krish, her senior stylist and an irrepressible gossip, Paul had been working on a high-profile case involving human traffickers and was making quite a name for himself.

"It's all thanks to you, Daisy," Krish had told her. "If you hadn't helped him crack the Levanté case, he'd still be doing the graveyard shift at the precinct."

She trimmed Liz's hair into a stylish bob, then blow-dried it. When she was done, Liz was back to her perfectly coiffed self.

"Fabulous, thanks, dear," she said, admiring herself in the mirror. She smoothed a hand over her cheek as if trying to iron out the wrinkles and gave a little sigh. "I'm going to call an Uber because I don't want to ruin it the moment I walk outside. I'm meeting with the mayor tomorrow about the congestion between Esher and Edgemead. Did I tell you?"

"Yes, I think you did mention it," said Daisy. "And take your time, there's no rush."

Liz paid the bill, and once she'd gone, Daisy set about straightening up her salon. She liked this time of day, after the last customer had left, because time seemed to slow down. Cleaning whilst listening to music had become something of an evening ritual. It helped her unwind after the frenetic pace of the day and gave her a chance to recharge her batteries after the constant chatter of her customers—not that she minded talking to them, but after eight solid hours, she needed a break. Krish had told her she was the only person he knew who actually liked cleaning, but she found it therapeutic.

"There," she said to herself, as she stood back to admire her handiwork. The salon was sparkling. The floors were clean, the mirrors shone, and she could see her reflection in the silver utensil trays.

The only problem was her missing scissors, she still hadn't found them. If they didn't turn up tomorrow, she'd have to rummage through the storeroom cupboard for another pair. She had backups, so it wasn't a train smash, but they were expensive and she wanted to find them. The vintage-style clock on the wall said it was almost nine o'clock. Time to go home.

Daisy glanced out of the shop window. It was still pelting down. The sound of the rain was drowned out by Cavalli, but she could see by the big, wide splatters that it was torrential.

"Darn rain," she muttered. Her car was at home so it would be a very wet ten-minute walk back to her cottage, and her umbrella—which had a nasty habit of inverting itself—would offer little protection in this wind.

She locked the front door from the inside and turned off the lights and the radio before walking through to the kitchenette at the back. Suddenly, the rain seemed inordinately loud. Suppressing a shiver, she pulled on her coat and gloves and grabbed her umbrella.

I'm going to get drenched, she thought as she opened the back door and sharp daggers of rain pierced her skin. Squinting, she opened her umbrella and stepped out into the deluge.

Here goes.

She locked the door behind her, then turned around and nearly fell over someone lying about a metre from the doorway. "What the . . . ?"

She bent down, immediately recognising the hair for she'd styled it herself only that morning. It was Melanie Haverstock, one of her customers! And she was lying in the sodden street with Daisy's missing scissors sticking out of her back.

Chapter Two

Detective Chief Inspector Paul McGuinness stood over the body of Melanie Haverstock, his tall, broad figure acting as a barrier against the driving rain. "What time did you find her?" he asked.

Daisy held her umbrella over her head, for all the good it was doing, and squinted up at him. "Nine o'clock."

"That's very precise."

"I checked the time when I locked up."

He nodded and turned his gaze back to the victim. She lay facedown in a growing puddle of rainwater, her newly styled hair resembling a sodden bird's nest, her navy-blue coat twisted around her stockinged legs. A crime scene photographer was documenting the position of the body, the murder weapon, and the rain-drenched alleyway. Daisy flinched as the pathologist carefully removed the scissors from between the victim's shoulder blades.

"I take it those belong to you?" The detective gestured toward the murder weapon.

She wrinkled her brow and said in a small voice, "They're my cutting scissors."

He sighed. "How is it you always seem to be connected to one of my victims?"

"Just lucky, I guess."

"This is serious, Daisy," he said, frowning.

"Of course, I'm sorry. I happen to know a lot of people in Edgemead," she pointed out. "Everybody comes into my salon at some point or another."

"Yes, so I've realised."

It was thanks to her local knowledge that he'd managed to solve the murder of the opera diva Dame Serena, the case that had kick-started his career.

Melanie was in her midthirties, plain but with a body that made up for it. Even at school, Melanie had matured before the rest of her year group, her ample breasts the envy of every schoolgirl and the focus of every teenage boy. Now, as an adult, she was still sexy with an hourglass figure and full, gravity-defying boobs that hadn't slumped even in death. Daisy strongly suspected they weren't her own.

"I take it you knew the victim?" It was more of a statement than a question.

"Yes, her name is Melanie Haverstock," Daisy replied. "She's one of my clients. In fact, she had an appointment this morning. Krish gave her a full colour makeover. She wanted—"

"What time was her appointment?" interrupted McGuinness, holding up a hand to cut her off. His face was so

wet, raindrops dripped off the end of his nose. He swiped
at it with the back of his hand in a futile attempt to halt
the deluge.

"I'll have to check my appointment book, but if memory serves, it was around ten o'clock."

He frowned. "If her appointment was this morning,
what was she doing outside the back door to your salon
this evening?"

"I don't know." Daisy had been wondering the same
thing. Even if Mel had wanted to speak to her about
something, why use the back door? It would be locked,
and it was doubtful she would have heard her from the
front of the salon.

"Was she a friend?" enquired McGuinness. "Would
she have come to meet you after work to go for a drink,
anything like that?"

"No," said Daisy. "I've known her for ages, we were at
school together, but we weren't close. I didn't see her so-
cially. As I said, she was a customer, but then almost everyone in the village is."

McGuinness ran a hand through his drenched hair,
slicking it back off his forehead. His raincoat was turned
up at the collar, and he was hunched forwards against the
cold. Daisy felt sorry for him. It was a horrid night to be
called out to a murder scene.

The forensic team was erecting a tent around the body
and asked them to stand back. "Do you want to come inside?" asked Daisy, since the rain didn't seem to be letting up.

McGuinness nodded. "Just for a minute."

Daisy pushed opened the back door to the salon and
they stood inside, watching the tent go up. "So, you can't
think of any reason why she came to see you tonight?"

Daisy shook her head. "No. Unless she was unhappy with her colour, but if that was the case, she'd have called or made another appointment."

There was a slight pause. The rain clattered on the roof negating the need for small talk.

Daisy thought back to the last time they'd seen each other, nearly six months ago. They'd met for lunch in Guildford, where he was based. She'd been excited to see him again, taken care with her appearance, styled her hair—things she hadn't done before meeting a man in a long time. A real date. It had made her feel excited, but nervous at the same time. Foreign feelings . . . or maybe not foreign, just long forgotten. This was new territory for her. Since Tim had up and left . . . Well, she hadn't gone on a date in years, so this was a big deal. She wasn't even sure what was happening between them, but it was definitely something, and for the first time in years, she wanted to see where it went.

Except it hadn't gone anywhere; instead it had fizzled out like a campfire in a rainstorm. No sooner had they ordered their drinks, than his phone had rung and he'd been called away to a crime scene, and just like that, her warm, fuzzy feeling had evaporated into the garlic-scented air. Oh, he'd apologised and promised to make up for it, but the days had turned into weeks and he still hadn't called. He was busy with his investigation—he was a detective chief inspector now—and to be fair, Paul wasn't the texting type. So, Daisy's life returned to normal, until Floria, her best friend, had invited her to the south of France on holiday. Daisy had taken three weeks off work and luxuriated in the sun, determined to put all thoughts of the tough, handsome detective out of her head.

Then he'd called.

She'd been lying on the beach reading a fashion magazine when she'd heard her phone buzz in the beach bag beside her. Looking down, she'd seen McGuinness's name appear on the screen. After staring at it for a long moment, she'd let it go to voicemail. It was better that way. He hadn't called again.

"Was she married?" he asked, breaking her reverie.

"Who?"

He gave her a strange look. "The victim, Melanie Haverstock."

"Oh, sorry. Yes, she was." She pulled her brain back to the present. The rain was so loud she had to shout to be heard. "Her husband's name is Douglas. He's an accountant, but I'm not sure where he works. He keeps to himself."

McGuinness pulled a damp notebook out of his raincoat pocket and made a note. "And when you saw Melanie this morning, was she upset or distressed? Did she appear to be herself?"

Daisy thought back to earlier that day. She'd been busy with three of Penny's friends who'd come in to have their hair done for the hen party and hadn't given much thought to Melanie. "Krish did her colour, he's a genius at that, but as far as I could tell, she seemed her normal self. You'll have to ask him, though. He'll be in tomorrow."

"You're open on Sundays?"

"Only in the morning, for those customers who can't make it during the week. We take it in turns."

"I see." He gave her a sideways glance and shuffled

his feet. "Look, Daisy, I'm sorry I haven't been in touch," he began.

She shook her head. "It's okay, I understand. You've been busy."

He paused, then nodded. It was easier that way. Neither of them needed the complication of a relationship. He didn't have the time, and she, well, she wasn't sure it was the right thing for her after all. All that emotional angst, who needed it? Luckily, Sergeant Buckley arrived and destroyed any chance of further private conversation.

"Sorry I'm late," panted McGuinness's sidekick, coming to a halt in a giant puddle in front of the door. "There was a pileup on the M3." He had an earnest, flat face, and it was clear he was a little bit afraid of his DCI, despite having worked for him for over a year. In all the time she'd known him, Daisy had yet to see him smile.

The tent was up within minutes and the interior illuminated by portable strip-lights. DCI McGuinness nodded to his sergeant, and they went inside, closing the flap behind them.

Daisy hesitated, then raising the flap, snuck in behind them. She'd already seen the body, anyway.

"You shouldn't be in here," McGuinness said without looking up. He knew she'd follow them in.

"I see her handbag is still there," Daisy pointed out as if he hadn't spoken. Melanie's black leather purse was zipped shut, the metallic strap coiled on the ground beside her where she'd dropped it when she fell. "It doesn't look like a mugging."

McGuinness shot her a sideways glance. "Yes, I can see that. Thank you, Daisy."

Turning his back on her, he pulled a pair of latex

gloves from his pocket and put them on, before bending down to open the victim's bag. "Mobile phone is here," he remarked, inspecting it briefly before putting it back. "Wallet, perfume. Nothing appears to be taken. Let's get hold of her phone records and see who she was talking to before she was killed."

Buckley nodded.

Daisy got a whiff of the expensive perfume Melanie had been wearing that morning. She swallowed, her mouth suddenly dry. It was eerie smelling her scent, knowing she was dead.

Two forensic officers turned Melanie over. Daisy's first instinct was to look away, but she forced herself to focus on the victim's face. It was wet and pasty, with an abnormal plastic sheen that reminded her of the wax-works at Madame Tussauds. Melanie's jersey dress had soaked up a lot of rain, turning it charcoal grey instead of its previous dove grey.

"She's not wearing the same clothes," Daisy blurted out. "She was in black leggings and a mustard-yellow jumper this morning. It is the same jacket, though."

"You remember what she was wearing?" DCI McGuinness looked surprised. "I thought you said she was Krish's customer."

"She was, but I'm very observant. Besides, the mustard-yellow went really well with her new hair colour. Set it off nicely." The detective barely refrained from rolling his eyes. She couldn't blame him; he was a man's man. There was nothing remotely effeminate about him. His hulking frame was intimidating, and he had big hands, big feet, and a broad chest, although he seemed to have put on a little bit of weight since she'd seen him last. She guessed it was the result of working too hard and consuming too many takeaways. She'd gotten to know him a little during the Dame Serena case last year. He played rugby for a local club but only when he got the chance, he lived alone—although to be fair, she didn't know if that was still the case—and he liked to watch sport to relax. Hair and nail maintenance was probably as alien to him as motorcar maintenance was to her.

"Would you say this is a smart outfit?" he asked Daisy, his gaze on the victim's attire.

She glanced up. "Yes, it's smarter than what she was wearing earlier today, anyway."

"Do you think she was on her way to meet someone?"

Daisy studied the figure-hugging jersey dress, the stockings, and the high-heeled shoes, then her gaze shifted to her face. "Unlikely," she said. "Her makeup has come off, and she hasn't bothered to reapply it. Smudged eyeliner. No lipstick. I think it's more likely she met with someone earlier in the day before she was killed."

McGuinness scratched his chin. "Any idea who?"

"Hmm . . . not really. She was treasurer of the Women's Institute, so she may have been seeing someone regarding that, I don't know. She could have been meeting a friend or an associate, I suppose." Did Mel even have female friends? Daisy didn't know anyone she was particularly close to, but then she didn't know her that well.

He nodded at Buckley. "Look into that, will you?"

"Perhaps her phone records will tell us," said Buckley.

"Time of death?" McGuinness asked the pathologist, who was leaning over the body.

"I'd say in the last hour, so between eight and nine this evening," he replied. "She's still warm."

Poor Mel. Daisy hadn't liked her much, but to die like

this, in a back alley? She shivered and wrapped her arms around herself. Who'd want to do this to her? And why use Daisy's cutting scissors to do it?

DCI McGuinness cleared his throat. "Daisy, I'm sorry to have to do this, but would you mind coming with me to the station to give a statement?"

Daisy stared at him. "What, now?" It was pitch dark, late as hell, and she was exhausted. Surely the statement could wait until a more reasonable hour.

He nodded. "If you wouldn't mind."

She held his gaze for a short while, then the realisation struck. "Am I a suspect now?"

He looked away. "No, of course not, but it was your scissors that killed her, and you were the one who discovered the body."

"I was also the one who called you," she insisted. "Come on, Paul."

He spread his hands. "I'm sorry, Daisy. It's procedure, you know that. I have to take you in. Once we take your fingerprints, we can eliminate you from our inquiries."

"I know how it works." She sighed. Her second-year criminology diploma had explained the arrest procedure in detail. Basically, it was apprehend any suspects first, ask questions later. And McGuinness had to be seen to be doing his job. "You're serious?"

He nodded.

"Okay, let me get my purse. I've left it in the kitchen."

"Do you mind if we take your gloves?" asked Sergeant Buckley, after a nod from his boss.

"Um, sure." She took off her woolen gloves and handed them to Buckley, who held out an evidence bag. She dropped them inside.

"You didn't touch the body, did you?" asked McGuinness, almost as an afterthought.

"No, I don't think so. I mean, I almost tripped over her when I left the salon, but I didn't bend down and touch her. I called you straightaway."

"Okay, good. There shouldn't be any problem, then."

Daisy didn't like the sound of that.

"We're ready to take her away," said a paramedic, and for a fleeting moment Daisy thought they meant her, then she realised they were talking about the body.

"My car is out front," DCI McGuinness said, taking off down the alleyway.

Daisy grabbed her purse, locked the back door, then followed him to his car. She had to run to keep up. Buckley kept a sharp eye on her, which was a tad annoying. It wasn't like she was going to make a run for it.

She knew she had to give a statement, but to escort her to the station tonight under police guard and take her gloves as evidence . . .

She was a suspect. There was no denying it. Someone was framing her for the murder of Melanie Haverstock. But who? And why?

Chapter Three

Daisy sat in the back of DCI McGuinness's black BMW feeling like a common criminal. Any lingering attraction she'd felt for him had dissolved into one of the muddy puddles on the motorway. Being carted off to the police station by the man you secretly fancied was kind of a passion killer. Even their past connection seemed like a fragment of her imagination.

Daisy sighed. At least he hadn't turned on the blue flashing lights. That would have been more than she could bear. DS Buckley, who was sitting up front with him, shot her furtive glances in the rearview mirror.

"You know it wasn't me," she huffed, as McGuinness opened up on the motorway heading toward Guildford. The night scenery sped by in a blur of open fields and silvery lakes. It was still raining, and the windscreen wipers whipped back and forth, grating on her nerves. "Why would I kill Melanie Haverstock? She was a client of mine."

Paul kept his eyes on the road. "It doesn't matter what I think, Daisy. We still have to do this by the book. You're a person of interest in this case, and I have to take you in for questioning. Don't make it any harder than it has to be."

He was just doing his job, she knew that, and he was nothing if not thorough. "By the Book" ought to be his middle name. Paul "By the Book" McGuinness. Her shoulders slumped and she leaned back against the plush leather seats, her mind racing. There had been so many people in the salon that day, any one of them could have stolen her cutting scissors.

That was the first question DCI McGuinness asked her under caution.

"Well, we opened at nine as usual, and my first customer was Ruth from the doctor's surgery. She comes in twice a week to have her hair straightened. I give her a special deal because she's a regular. Poor woman's terrified of the rain, so this weather's a nightmare for her. It turns her frizzy hair into an Afro, which is not a good look for her."

DS Buckley cast a worried glance at his boss.

"Does she know Melanie Haverstock?" the DCI asked, getting back to the point.

"Probably," said Daisy. "Everybody goes to the doctor at some point, don't they? In fact, Ruth probably knows a lot of embarrassing secrets about most of the residents in Edgemead."

He sighed. "Okay, who was next?"

"Mrs. Robbins came in for her usual Saturday rinse

and set. Krish took care of her, they like to fill each other in on the town gossip. She lives in the sheltered housing complex near the high street and is a sweet old lady with blue hair and no motive whatsoever. In fact, I don't think she even knew the victim."

"Right."

Buckley made notes as she spoke, while McGuinness fixed his grey eyes on her, keeping his expression neutral.

"Then, I had two hours booked out for the hen party."

At his confused look, she elaborated. "Paloma, Apple, and Ferne, friends of Penny, my other stylist, came in to have their hair done for the hen party tonight. Paloma's getting married tomorrow. I did all three of them myself, so I booked out a two-hour slot. They drank a lot of champagne and were generally quite excitable, but I don't know if any of them knew Melanie. Oh, and I definitely had my scissors then, because I gave Ferne and Apple a trim. They had a load of split ends, thanks to all that styling for their modelling shoots. The heat plays havoc with your hair."

DS Buckley scribbled something on his notepad. Daisy wondered if he even knew what a split end was. He looked like he'd been born with a short, military-style buzz cut.

They were sitting in a stark interview room in the bowels of the Guildford Police Station. It was cold and the fluorescent lights were overly bright, probably to make the suspect, or statement-giver in her case, as uncomfortable as possible. Their conversation, or rather interview, was being recorded. The button on the electrical device flashed green to show it was in use. Daisy had no legal representation; she'd waived her right. Why did she need a solicitor when she was innocent? She genuinely wanted to help the police with their enquiries. It was in her best interests that they caught the real killer so Daisy could clear her name.

"That was when Krish was doing Mel's colour job," Daisy added as an afterthought. "Penny was seeing to another of our regulars, Soraya Patel. Her husband owns the newsagent across the road. She has the most gorgeous, glossy black hair that hardly ever needs anything done to it, just a quick trim every now and then."

More scribbling by Buckley. DCI McGuinness studied her across the stainless-steel table. His large hands were clasped casually in front of him, but she could tell by his forward stance and rigid jawline that he was uneasy. Well, this wasn't very pleasant for her either.

"If you could stick to the facts, please, Miss Thorne."

Oh, so she was "Miss Thorne" now, was she? That was for the benefit of the recording. She glared at him and sat back in her chair. The cold metal seeped through her damp blouse, and she supressed a shiver. They'd taken her coat as soon as she'd arrived at the police station. Placing it in another see-through bag, no doubt to check for Melanie's DNA. Well, good luck to them. She could save everyone the trouble and tell them they wouldn't find anything and they were just wasting their time, but they wouldn't listen. Paul would insist. She could hear his voice loud and clear in her head. "*We have to follow protocol, Daisy*," he would say.

Ugh, now the man was in her head.

"Who was next?" asked Buckley, getting the interview back on track, his pen poised over his notepad.

Daisy tried to think back to earlier in the day. This would have been a lot easier if she'd thought to bring her appointment book, but then they'd probably confiscate that too, and she needed it to keep track of her customers. "At twelve o'clock, I left to meet my friend Donna Levanté for lunch. You might remember her, Detective? You met last year when we solved her mother's murder together."

That was for the benefit of the tape too. Donna was Floria's half sister and fast becoming a good friend of Daisy's.

It was Paul's turn to scowl. He brought out the steely, thousand-yard stare that had intimidated so many of his suspects, of which she was now one. It didn't perturb her. He might act like the ruthless detective, but deep down, he was a decent guy. Not that she knew him well, but in those rare off-duty moments they'd spent together, she'd caught a glimpse of the real Paul. The man behind the detective mask. The man that nobody, not even his colleagues or coworkers, saw. As his grey eyes shot lasers across the table, she had to give him credit, he knew how to act the part. Not wanting him to stare holes through her, Daisy shifted her gaze to the one-way glass mirror behind him. Dark and reflective, she wondered if anyone was standing behind it now, watching this interview.

"What time did you get back?" This from Buckley again.

"At one o'clock, then I washed and blow-dried Donna's hair. Or rather, Asa washed, and I blow-dried. Asa's our washer, although she's doing nails now too."

McGuinness sighed; the fingers clenched, then unclenched again. Daisy ignored him. "Donna had a performance last night at the Southbank Theatre. Unfortunately, I couldn't make it." Donna was first violin in the London Symphony Orchestra. She'd worked hard to get there, and Daisy was extremely proud of her.

"Did you have your scissors at that point?" questioned McGuinness.

Daisy bit her lip and racked her brains. Did she? "You know, I can't remember. I didn't need them for Donna, so I wouldn't have noticed if they were missing or not."

"Did you use them again that afternoon?" he pressed.

"That's a really good question, Detective. I had a few ladies from the retirement home near Esher come in—they get the charity bus that brings them into town—but Penny and Krish helped me and there were scissors lying all over the countertop, so I could have used someone else's." She shrugged helplessly. "I'm sorry, I know that's not very useful."

"I appreciate you're trying to help, Miss Thorne. So, when was the first time you noticed your scissors missing?"

"Only later that evening," Daisy told him. "When Liz Roberts came in. That was when I first noticed they weren't in my drawer."

"Do you always put them back?" Buckley asked.

"Yes, or someone else does. Mine has my initials scraped into the side, it's how we tell our scissors apart. Asa usually sweeps up before she leaves at five, but we try to keep the place clean after every customer, so anyone could have picked up my scissors during the course of the afternoon."

DCI McGuinness turned to Buckley. "Does the murder weapon have Miss Thorne's initials on them?"

"I'll go and check." He excused himself for the purposes of the tape.

Paul rubbed his eyes; he looked tired. Daisy was also beginning to feel the strain of the evening's drama. She yawned, which Paul caught, and his jaw worked as he tried to stifle it. She managed a weak smile. "How much longer are we going to be?"

"Not long."

He glanced at the file on the table. Daisy knew it to be the murder docket he'd opened for Melanie Haverstock. Her name would be in there, at the top of the suspect list.

"Could you please give me the full names of your staff members?" he said.

"You know who they are," she retorted.

He scowled at her. "For the recording."

Daisy sighed audibly. "Alright. Krishna Ranganathan is my head stylist, although he goes by Krish. He's a genius with colour and . . ."

"Just their names, please. I don't need their biographies as well."

Another sigh.

"Penny Whitely is my other senior stylist. Then there's Bianca, a young Polish girl who comes in twice a week. I'm training her. Her surname is Woźniak, but I'm not entirely sure which letter the accent goes on."

McGuinness wrote the name at the bottom of Buckley's notepad. His handwriting was more of an illegible scribble, whereas Buckley printed his notes, which made them easier to read upside down.

"Asa Gordon-Smith is my washer and nail technician." She resisted the urge to inform the tape and whoever was listening in the viewing room about Asa's talents in the nail department. They wouldn't care.

"And then there's me, the owner. Daisy Thorne." She fixed her gaze on him. He held it for a split second, before glancing down at his file.

"Thank you, Miss Thorne."

Buckley came back into the room and resumed his

seat. McGuinness turned to him expectantly. Buckley nodded.

McGuinness sighed.

Daisy wasn't surprised. She'd known the minute she'd seen them that it was her scissors that had killed Melanie, but McGuinness had obviously been hoping otherwise. He gave her a concerned look as he said out loud, "DS Buckley has just confirmed that the murder weapon is indeed Miss Thorne's hairdressing scissors."

The atmosphere in the room became heavy. Buckley sat upright in his chair, his awkward gaze fixed on his notepad; McGuiness drummed his fingers on the table, frown lines etched on his brow; and Daisy waited for someone to say something.

"Okay," McGuinness said finally. "Let's go over your movements between eight and nine p.m. this evening."

Although she'd already told him what she'd done, Daisy knew this was important evidence that had to go on the record. The problem was, she didn't have anyone to back up her statement, and that meant she didn't have an alibi for the full hour. Well, it couldn't be helped. Just because she didn't have an alibi, didn't mean she was a murderer. In fact, most innocent people didn't have alibis because they didn't need them. It was only the guilty who were obsessed with proving their innocence.

"I finished Mrs. Roberts's hair at eight thirty-five or thereabouts. She called an Uber because it was raining and she didn't want to ruin her new hairdo. I swept the floor while she waited for it to arrive. Shortly after that, she left and I wiped the countertops and polished the mirrors before locking up for the night." Her evening routine.

"You locked the front door?"

"Yes, after Liz left, I locked the front door and hung up the CLOSED sign, like I do every evening."

"And you heard nothing out of the ordinary? No shouts or screams?"

She shook her head. "No, but that's not surprising since it was bucketing down with rain, which always makes a racket on the corrugated kitchen roof. Plus, the back door was thumping in the wind." She also had Cavalli blaring through the salon, but she didn't mention that. The foul weather meant she wouldn't have heard anything, anyway.

"What time did you leave the salon?"

"A few minutes after nine o'clock. I checked the time, then put on my coat and gloves, grabbed my umbrella, and went out the back." Had she forgotten anything? She didn't think so.

"And that's when you found Mrs. Haverstock's body?"

"Yes, I didn't immediately notice her lying there because of the driving rain. I locked the door behind me and turned around, and that's when I saw her."

"You said you nearly tripped over her?"

"That's right, yes. I wasn't expecting to find a dead body outside my back door, so it took me by surprise."

"Let's be very clear on this next point, Daisy." His voice softened as he said her first name. Her eyes flew to his face, and she saw how important this question was. He was worried, she could read it as clear as day on his face. For the first time since she'd arrived at the police station, Daisy felt a frisson of fear. It didn't matter that he knew she hadn't done it. All the evidence pointed to her, and that meant that McGuinness's hands were tied. Her criminology diploma had taught her that. Melanie had been *her* client, killed with *her* scissors, which were bound to have *her* fingerprints on them, right outside *her* salon. It didn't get more cut-and-dried than that. Based on the evidence, it was remarkable he hadn't arrested her already. "You didn't touch the body?"

Daisy held his gaze. "No, like I told you before, I did not touch her. I called the emergency services straightaway, after which I phoned you. Then I went back inside the salon until they came."

McGuinness had arrived about half an hour later, having raced through from Guildford. Because Edgemead didn't have a police station of its own, thanks to recent budget cuts, they now fell under the jurisdiction of Guildford, the nearest large town.

The police had cordoned off the alleyway to preserve the crime scene by the time he'd gotten there, and Daisy had kept out of the way so as not to contaminate the scene. Hopefully, there would be some clues on or around the body that could point the police in the direction of her killer, although given the torrential rain, she didn't think that was very likely.

"Okay, fine. Well, I think that's all for now. Thanks for coming in to give your statement, Miss Thorne. We appreciate it."

Like she'd had a choice in the matter. She nodded and stood up.

"This interview is terminated at"—McGuinness consulted his watch—"seven minutes past twelve." Buckley switched off the recording.

Daisy exhaled and stretched her neck to relieve some of the stress. She'd never been interviewed by the police before. It wasn't fun. "Can I go now?"

"Yes, but we may need to talk to you again, pending

the results of the DNA tests." She glanced up, momentarily confused, then she remembered her jacket and gloves.

"I understand." At least he hadn't told her not to leave town or anything as clichéd as that. "Buckley will see you out." He gave her a curt nod but couldn't hide his concern.

She walked past him, her head held high, determined not to let him see how rattled she was. If all they had in that manila file was her name, then she was in real trouble. The sooner she could get to the bottom of this murder, the better.

Chapter Four

Daisy woke up and groaned. Light flooded through her bedroom window, spotlighting her in its blinding glow. She'd been so exhausted when she'd gotten home last night that she'd forgotten to draw the blinds. A taxi had finally dropped her off around 1 a.m. That was the problem with the police, she mused. They were quite happy to take you in for questioning, but they sure as hell weren't going to offer you a lift home afterwards.

Feeling edgy and out of sorts, she turned over and snuggled under the covers, trying to ignore her bright surroundings and go back to sleep. It didn't work. Now that she was awake, the events of last night penetrated her groggy consciousness, and it was impossible not to think about them.

Poor Melanie. She'd been so happy with her new hair

colour; it had really suited her too. Despite their differ-
ences, it had warmed Daisy's heart to see the woman's
confident swagger as she'd left the salon. Another happy
customer.

Now she was lying cold and lifeless in the morgue.
Daisy shivered and sat up. There was no point in fretting.
She might as well get up, make a coffee, and start thinking about launching her own investigation. She pictured
DCI McGuinness's austere face and imagined him shaking his head, then just as quickly, she pushed the image
from her mind. This was *her* life on the line; *she* was the
primary suspect.

The first person Daisy wanted to talk to was Penny, her
senior stylist and the last staff member to leave the salon
last night, other than her. Glancing at the time, she wondered whether she'd make it to Penny's before she left for
the wedding. Paloma, Penny's model friend, was getting
married today, and Penny was a bridesmaid.

It was eight o'clock. If she remembered correctly, the
wedding was at eleven, which meant Penny would probably be up and starting to get ready. If she left now, she
should catch her alone. It wouldn't be long before
McGuinness tracked her down, either.

Penny lived in a modern clump of townhouses just
outside of Edgemead. The quaint two-up and two-down
property was new and well-maintained. The gardens were
landscaped, and the roads were all clearly marked with
ample parking out front.

Daisy knocked on Penny's door. The doormat squelched
beneath her feet, and the lawn glistened from last night's
downpour, but at least it had stopped raining. Penny
opened it wearing a towelling robe.

"Daisy, what are you doing here?"

"Can I come in?" asked Daisy, pleased that she'd gotten here before the police. Penny still didn't know what had happened.

"Of course. I'm getting ready, so you'll have to excuse me, but come in."

Daisy followed her into the neat hallway and up a flight of stairs to her bedroom. The bridesmaid's dress, a lavender, floor-length creation with three-quarter sleeves, hung on the wardrobe. Beneath it was a pair of sparkly lavender heels.

"Gorgeous dress," commented Daisy, moving Penny's nightdress and a pair of sheer stockings out of the way so she could sit on the bed.

"Yes, although it clashes terribly with my hair," she complained.

Daisy chuckled. Penny was a flaming redhead with pale, flawless skin. That, along with her even features, witchy-green eyes, and exquisite bone structure, was the reason Penny was so successful as a model, even though it was more of a side hustle than her main source of income.

Still, she did one or two magazine shoots every month, and it was a nice little side-earner for her. When Daisy had asked her why she didn't model full-time, Penny had winced. "Why would I want to do that? It's a cut-throat business, Daisy, and I'm not built for it."

Despite her head-turning looks, Penny wasn't the extroverted type. She preferred a secure, stable job and a small, close-knit group of friends. Paloma was the one exception. Daisy had never quite figured out why they were friends, but she didn't question it. Penny must have her reasons.

"How are you wearing it?" Daisy asked.

"I thought up, in a chignon. That way it minimises the redness."

"I can do it, if you'd like?" Daisy offered.

"Oh, would you? That would be great. I washed it last night, so it's clean."

"Take a seat at the dresser," Daisy said. "I'll do it now, before you get dressed."

"Fab, you're a darling." Penny sat down and glanced at Daisy's reflection. "What was it you wanted to speak to me about?"

Daisy took a deep breath. This would come as a shock, but her colleague needed to know. "Melanie Haverstock was murdered last night."

"No!" Penny gasped and spun around so fast Daisy took a step back. "How?"

"That's the worrying part. I found her body outside the back door to the salon. She was stabbed with my cutting scissors!"

Penny gaped at her, mouth open, eyes wide with shock. "Oh. My. Gosh."

"I know. Guess who the main suspect is?"

Penny stared at her, horrified. "They can't honestly suspect you, Daisy?" She hesitated. "Can they?"

"Oh, they can, and they do," Daisy retorted. "I spent the better part of last night at the Guildford Police Department, courtesy of my buddy, DCI McGuinness."

"But he knows you wouldn't kill anyone. You dated him, for heaven's sake."

"We went out once," Daisy clarified. "That doesn't count as dating."

Penny shrugged. "Close enough."

"Anyway, he had to follow protocol. I did find the body, after all."

Penny frowned, clearly perturbed. "I don't understand, Dais. Why would someone kill Melanie with your cutting scissors?"

That was the million-dollar question.

"I don't know," she whispered. "To frame me, maybe? To divert suspicion away from them."

"Does that mean it was one of our customers?" Penny's hand flew to her mouth. "It must be, mustn't it? Who else would steal your scissors?"

"Well, that's what I wanted to talk to you about. You didn't see them lying around anywhere, did you? Or put them somewhere? I last remember having them when I trimmed Ferne and Apple's hair yesterday morning, but we had a lot of people in and out during the day and I can't remember if I used them again after that."

Penny thought for a moment. "I may have done it," she said tentatively. "I tend to clear up automatically. You know how it is?"

Daisy did. They all did their bit. After each customer, the floor was swept, the surfaces were cleared, and any equipment was put away. They handled each other's stuff all the time.

She blew a stray hair out of her face. "That's the problem. If I could remember, then I'd have a better idea of who stole them."

"Who hates you enough to want to pin this on you?" Penny wondered.

"Good question. Although they might just want to throw suspicion off themselves and onto someone else, and I was the most convenient patsy." She hoped so, anyway. It gave her shivers thinking that this might be a personal vendetta. As far as she knew, nobody hated her that much.

"Let's make a list of all the customers we had that day," said Penny, swivelling to face the mirror. "And we'll go through them one by one."

"Good idea," agreed Daisy, who'd already done a mental version of that. Maybe seeing it in black and white would help. Penny grabbed an eyeliner and wrote the names on her mirror.

Okay, in brown and glass, then.

"It can't be Ruth because I had my scissors after her appointment," Daisy began, starting with her first customer of the day. "Krish had Mrs. Robbins, but she's a sweet old thing and wouldn't have the strength to stab someone in the back. As it is, we have to help her into the salon with her walker."

Penny wrote *Ruth* and *Mrs. Robbins* on the board but drew a line through each of their names. Next, she wrote *Paloma*, *Ferne*, and *Apple* in a row, next to each other. They'd all come in together for their two-hour appointment.

"Don't forget Mel and Soraya," said Daisy. Penny added their names to the list. They stared at it for a few moments. "Well, Mel wouldn't have taken them, she was the victim," Penny pointed out and drew a line through her name too.

"Unless she stole them and the murderer took them off her?" mused Daisy.

Penny tilted her head to the side. "You really think so?"

"No," said Daisy, after a short pause. That made even less sense. It would be better if they focused on the most obvious suspects first. "Not really. Let's cross her off the list."

"Did any of the models know Melanie?" Daisy asked Penny, who thought for a moment.

"I don't think so. They didn't mix in the same circles. Apple and Ferne stayed at the hotel in Esher with Paloma last night after the hen party, but they both live in north London. They're only in Surrey for Paloma's wedding, which is being held at the lodge in Richmond Park. I don't think they've even met Melanie."

"Except when they were in the salon at the same time," Daisy pointed out.

Penny gnawed on her lower lip. "They didn't speak to each other once. In fact, they weren't even aware of each other's presence. I don't think there's a connection there."

She was probably right. North London was a far cry from their little village of Edgemead, and trendy fashion models and WI treasurers were not mutually exclusive. Besides, the models were a good ten years younger than Melanie had been. And herself, since she'd been the same age as the victim, but she wasn't going to dwell on that.

"Were they at the hen party in Esher?" asked Daisy, moving on. Esher was a ten-minute drive from Edgemead in light traffic, but more like half an hour during the morning and afternoon rush.

"They were there when I arrived a few minutes after nine," said Penny. "A little worse for wear, but all three accounted for."

"Then we can rule them out," said Daisy, nodding at the mirror. Penny slashed through their names too. "The time of death was between eight and nine."

There was a pause as they both stared at the glass.

"That leaves us with Donna," said Daisy, a moment later. "I know she didn't kill Melanie because she was performing at the Southbank last night."

Another name with a line through it.

"The ladies from Fernwood House couldn't have done

it, either, because they left on the charity bus at five o'clock to return to the retirement home, and quite frankly, I can't see any of them wielding the cutting scissors over Melanie's back, can you?"

"No," mused Penny, hurriedly writing *Babs*, *Judy*, *Angie*, and *Yvonne* on the mirror, then drawing a squiggly line through all four of them.

"That takes us up to five o'clock. Asa and Krish left shortly after that, and I did Clayton from the library. He came in on the off chance there'd be a slot available. His sideburns were edging into Mr. Darcy territory. I think we can discount him. He looks after his elderly mother in the evenings once the carer's left. She can't do without him."

"And I did Zoe Blanc," said Penny. "She was a last-minute appointment, and I squeezed her in because she and her hubby were going out for supper to celebrate his birthday."

"That's easy enough to check," said Daisy, making a mental note to follow those up.

Penny put a question mark beside Clayton and Zoe's names.

"Then there's Liz Roberts," murmured Daisy, her gaze lingering on the distinguished woman's name. Apart from being head of the Edgemead WI and a formidable woman in her own right, Liz was on the board of several charities, and together with her dog-food billionaire husband, had many wealthy and well-connected friends.

Penny wrote her name on the board. "A question mark?" she asked.

"Yes, you'd better. Liz said she was getting an Uber on account of the rain, but I didn't actually see her get into it. I was tidying up when she left."

Another question mark next to Liz's name.

"Okay," said Penny. "And we know it wasn't one of us, so these are our chief suspects."

Daisy studied the mirror. Three names. Three people to check out.

She picked up a brush and began to comb through Penny's thick red locks. "I'll check Clayton out this afternoon. He lives with his mother at Raspberry Cottage, which is only two roads down from me. Zoe works at the bakery on Duke Street, so I'll pop in there on Monday morning."

"What about Liz?" asked Penny, positioning a bowl of hair pins in front of Daisy. Daisy took one and held it between her teeth while she rolled the hair around the brush and twisted it into shape.

"Liz is more difficult," said Daisy, through her teeth. She held the hair in place and secured it with a pin. Then she added a few more, expertly hiding them beneath the elegant twist. "I can't check with the Uber driver, they wouldn't give out that kind of information."

"You could ask her directly," suggested Penny, admiring the chignon. "That's great. Thanks, Daisy. It's so difficult reaching around to do it myself."

"I'm not finished yet." Daisy reached for the hair curler. "Can we plug this in?"

Penny did so, and they waited for it to heat up.

"I'll try," Daisy continued, "but we have to be careful with Liz. She's extremely well-connected. And I don't want to spook her. Right now, she's our strongest suspect."

The curler device beeped, and Daisy picked it up. She released a few tendrils from the side of Penny's face and wove them around the heated brush.

"You do realise the police are going to come knocking

at your door," she said, meeting her friend's eye in the mirror.

Penny started, her hand fluttering to her throat. "Oh my word. I hadn't thought of that."

"Hold still," said Daisy, not wanting to pull her hair out. "They'll ask you what time you left work yesterday evening, and what time you got to the hen party."

Penny paled. "I didn't go straight there. I went home to get changed because I was meeting Niall. I had a quick shower before I left for the party."

"I know," said Daisy. "You'll have to explain it to them. Did you see Niall?"

"No." Penny looked close to tears. "He cancelled because one of his prize mares went into labour."

Daisy sighed. Penny was going to have a hard time backing up her alibi. "Look, just tell them exactly what your movements were. I'll back you up, and I'm sure Niall will confirm about the mare."

Penny nodded. "Thank you, Daisy."

Daisy released the tendrils, which bounced back into position, then she did the same on the other side.

"There, perfect." She smiled. "You look gorgeous."

The buzzer on the front door rang. Penny glanced up in alarm.

Daisy peered out of the bedroom window, which overlooked the front porch. "Don't worry, it's only your fellow bridesmaids."

Penny exhaled, and went downstairs to let them in.

Daisy grabbed a wet wipe and hastily cleaned the eyeliner off the mirror. It left a dirty brown smudge. She was worried about Penny. Her senior stylist was next on the list of suspects, and like herself, Penny didn't have an alibi for the time of the murder. Hypothetically speaking,

Penny could have waited outside the back door of the salon for Melanie, then killed her using Daisy's scissors, and gone on to the hen party in Esher. Except Daisy knew she hadn't done that. Penny had been looking forward to seeing Niall all week, and she would have rushed home to shower and change before leaving for Esher. There was no way she'd have had time to do all that and kill Mel.

But would the police believe her?

Chapter Five

"**W**hy are you not dressed?" demanded Ferne, the maid of honour and head bridesmaid. She looked incredible in an identical lavender gown with a tiny, cinched-in waist. Goodness, she was thin.

"I'm sorry, that was my fault." Daisy smiled. "I came round to tell Penny about Melanie."

"Who's Melanie?" asked Apple, her blond hair piled up in a messy bun. It suited her. She had a sensual face with full lips and slanted violet eyes. It was easy to see why she was a model. Daisy had heard she came from money, and that her uncle, or one of her male relatives, was an earl.

"Melanie was a friend of ours who . . . who passed away yesterday."

"Oh, I'm sorry." Apple looked shocked.

Daisy glanced at Ferne, who didn't react at all. "Well, you'd better get a move on," she said to Penny. "The limo will be here in half an hour."

Daisy met Penny's eye. Neither of them appeared to know who Melanie was. Oh well, it had been worth a shot.

Penny took her bridesmaid's dress off the hanger. "Does anyone feel like some champers?" she asked. "I've got a bottle in the fridge."

"Yes!" they all sang in unison.

"I'll get it." Daisy headed for the stairs.

"The flutes are in the cupboard to the right," Penny called after her.

When Daisy returned with the champagne and four glasses, Penny was stepping into her gown. She handed the bottle to Ferne and put the glasses on the dresser. "Here, let me help you zip it up."

Penny sucked in her stomach as Daisy did up the zip. "Heavens, how did you fit into this, Ferne?" asked Penny, gasping for air. "I can hardly breathe, and you had a smaller size than Apple and me."

"I don't eat," said Ferne simply.

Daisy raised an eyebrow. "That's not good. I hope you won't pass out during the service."

"Not all of us are lucky enough to be naturally thin." Ferne handed Daisy a glass of bubbly.

Daisy accepted it and took a much-needed sip. Sure, it was only nine thirty in the morning, but the fruity bubbles tasted delicious, and after the trauma of last night, she could use a lift.

The mood lightened, and soon the girls were giggling and gossiping as Penny expertly applied her makeup.

Daisy sat on the bed and listened as they proceeded to slag off everybody they knew.

"Did you see Delores in those leopard-print leggings at the casting last weekend?" Ferne said. "She's easily put on a stone since the Milan shoot."

"I hear she's seeing that Italian DJ, D-Tox. He's at all her shows." Apple fanned herself. "What a hottie. He doesn't seem to mind her curves."

"Boyfriends make you fat," snapped Ferne, then cast a knowing glance at Penny. "Careful you don't balloon now you're with Niall, Pen."

Penny patted her flat stomach. "Tell me about it. It's the dining out that gets you. All those creamy dressings and bottles of wine."

Ferne sniffed. "Thankfully, I don't have to worry about that."

Daisy secretly thought Penny had blossomed since she'd been dating Niall. The additional weight made her even prettier, but she was by no means fat. It just knocked off the bony edges, that was all.

"I put on half a stone when I was with Daniel," confessed Apple, running her hands over her smooth hips. "But luckily I've lost it all now. He had a nasty habit of ordering pizza whenever he came over."

"Did you break up with him?" Ferne raised an eyebrow.

"Of course not. Nothing that dramatic. I just banned him from eating pizza in front of me."

Daisy very much doubted that pizza ever touched either of these girls' lips; in fact, they probably didn't even get within sniffing distance.

"Are you doing the spring fleur fashion show in February?" Apple asked Penny. "I heard a rumour you'd been signed."

Penny sighed. "Yes, I wasn't sure if I wanted to, but it's good money and I do love her designs. The spring collection is bound to be stunning. How about you?"

"No, I'm doing Karl von Tonder instead. I can't do both."

Ferne downed the rest of her champagne and reached for the bottle to refill her glass. "Don't worry, Ferne," Apple said. "Something will come up. The agencies always take on more girls for the spring season."

"I know," Ferne said in a tight, little voice, but Daisy didn't miss the anxious expression that flashed across her face.

Daisy gazed from one to the other. They were all so beautiful and glamorous. Apple with her angelic looks and posh voice, Ferne with her dark, pixie-like beauty and waif-like frame, and Penny, the striking redhead. Gifted in the looks department, they made Daisy feel like a dowdy hag in comparison—and she was willing to bet she was curvier than Delores, whoever she might be.

After listening to them gabber away for ten more minutes, she could quite understand why Penny didn't want to be a part of this overly critical, backstabbing world. Didn't they have a nice thing to say about anybody?

"I think I'll leave you to it," she said, getting to her feet.

"Here's the limo," shouted Apple, peering out of the window. "Crumbs, it's massive."

Penny spritzed herself with perfume, and they floated downstairs on a cloud of Chanel. It was only after the limo had left, and Daisy was driving away in her VW, that she saw DCI McGuinness's BMW swoop up the street.

She smiled. He'd have a hard time tracking Penny down at the wedding. Her friend was safe until Monday morning.

Following up on the leads she and Penny had discussed, Daisy drove to Raspberry Cottage, Clayton's quaint house that he shared with his elderly mother. She parked in the lane outside and got out, inhaling deep breaths of fresh country air tainted by the mulchy leaves and the faint aroma of log fires.

Being Sunday, the residential village roads were quiet and the only activity was the herd of cows grazing in the meadow that sat between Clayton's street and her own. A big Friesian poked its wet nose through a hole in the fence and mooed at her. Daisy jumped.

"Hello," she said, as she locked the car. "You scared me."

She crossed the road and climbed the few steps to Clayton's front door. It was a glossy dark blue, with a shiny silver knocker in the middle of it, about head height. She knocked.

Clayton opened the door in a pair of Christmas pyjamas. Daisy glanced down. His feet were covered in elf slippers.

"Oh, hello, Daisy. I wasn't expecting company. What a surprise."

Daisy ignored his footwear and gave him a bright smile. "Sorry to disturb you, Clayton, but would you mind if I asked you a few questions?"

He wrinkled his forehead. "About what?"

"About last night. I don't know if you've heard, but Melanie Haverstock was killed outside the salon. The police took me in for questioning."

He gasped. He looked at her as if he wasn't sure whether she was joking or not. When she didn't react, he uttered, "Oh my gosh. Seriously?"

She nodded.

"Did you find the body?"

Daisy nodded again.

He glanced towards his mother, a slim, fragile figure with silvery-grey hair sitting in an armchair, a blanket over her lap. Her eyes were fixed on the television.

"Come in, but excuse the mess. We're watching reruns of *Britain's Got Talent*. This is the episode where that women threw eggs at the judges, do you remember it? It has me in stitches every time."

"Um, no." Daisy glanced at the television, where a man in a tuxedo was wiping egg off his face. Thank goodness it was on mute.

"It's a good one," he told her, ushering her into the room.

"Hello, Mrs. Beech." Daisy smiled at the elderly woman.

"Who are you?" she demanded.

Daisy raised her eyebrows, taken aback. She'd done Clayton's mother's hair countless times over the years, particularly when she'd first opened the salon.

"She's not too well," Clayton confided, then mouthed the word *dementia*.

Daisy nodded and sat down.

"When did this happen?" he asked. "Was it after my appointment yesterday afternoon?"

"It happened just before closing," Daisy confided. "I was locking up when I found her in the alley."

"Oh, Daisy, that's awful." He stared at her through his

bespectacled, beady eyes. With his greying hair and lean, slightly stooped frame, he was exactly how Daisy expected a librarian to look.

"Did you know her well?" Daisy asked.

Clayton frowned. "Not really. I mean, she came into the library every now and then, but mostly to use the printer. Her husband was the real reader. He had a taste for thrillers, particularly of the serial killer variety, in large print. I don't think his eyesight was very good."

"Thrillers, really?" She hadn't thought Douglas the type to read about serial killers for entertainment. He was so mild-mannered and nonconfrontational.

"Oh yes, he ploughed through them. Sometimes I ordered them in for him."

"Who's a serial killer?" asked Mrs. Beech.

"Nobody, Mother," Clayton replied, rolling his eyes. "She picks up bits and pieces."

"Who's in bits and pieces?" she said.

Clayton ignored her. "Poor Douglas, he must be devastated. He adored Melanie."

Interesting that he would sympathise with Douglas when Melanie was the one who'd been murdered. "I'm going over there shortly to offer my condolences," Daisy said.

"Please send him my best," said Clayton.

Daisy nodded. "Of course." She hesitated, then said, "I gave DCI McGuinness a list of all my customers. I'm sorry, Clayton, but you can expect a visit from the police in due course. I thought I'd give you a heads-up."

"That's okay, Daisy." To her surprise, he broke into a sly grin. "I don't mind having a cosy chat with that handsome detective of yours, even if it is as a potential suspect."

Daisy sighed. Did everyone in the neighbourhood think that she and DCI McGuinness were an item?

"He's not 'my' detective."

"Oh, tosh. Everybody knows he likes you." He winked at her. Daisy couldn't help but smile. Clayton, like Krish, was same-sex-oriented, although unlike Krish, his mother had never minded that her only son was gay. Quite the contrary, for it meant he hadn't got married and left home.

Krish, on the other hand, had been disowned by his family when he'd come out. That's why he'd relocated to Edgemead, in the southernmost corner of Surrey. He'd told Daisy his only thought was to get as far away from Wembley as possible, and he was relatively confident his parents would never set foot outside the M25.

"He'll want to know what your movements were last night," Daisy said, hedging.

"I was here, wasn't I, Mother?" He turned to the old lady, who hadn't taken her eyes off the television, despite the lack of sound.

"Serves him right," mumbled the old woman.

Not the most reliable alibi in the world, Daisy mused, although it was plain that Clayton's mother couldn't be left alone. She wondered what time the carer had left.

"She doesn't take much in these days," Clayton said to Daisy. "The Alzheimer's is quite advanced now."

"I'm so sorry." Daisy knew how close they were. "It can't be easy."

"We have a carer during the week, thankfully," he said with a little sigh. "It's the weekends that I find most try-ing. I will have to put her in a home soon." His face fell, and for a moment he appeared close to tears. Daisy patted his arm. Apart from a stint with a boyfriend that hadn't worked out, Clayton had lived with his mother as far back as Daisy could remember. She wasn't sure what had happened to his father; it had always just been Clayton and his mum.

"I'm only around the corner if you ever want to pop round for a cup of tea and a chat," she said.

He squeezed her hand. "Thanks, Daisy. You're a true friend."

Chapter Six

Since she had the car out, Daisy decided to visit Melanie's husband, Douglas, to give him her condolences. From what she could remember, he was a timid man with thinning hair and ratlike eyes. Quite unremarkable, really, considering his wife was such an extrovert. Melanie had prided herself on her figure, and while she hadn't been blessed in the looks department, she'd made up for it by sashaying around the village in high heels and tight clothing, setting off all the elderly gents' pacemakers.

"I'm so sorry for your loss," Daisy said, once Douglas had answered the door and invited her inside. His eyes were even redder than normal as if he'd been crying, and Daisy's heart went out to him.

"Would you like some tea?" he asked.

Daisy nodded. "Yes, thank you. That would be nice." She followed him into the kitchen. The sink was piled high with dirty dishes, and there was a pungent half-eaten pizza on the table.

Douglas took two mugs out of a cupboard and boiled the kettle. "Sorry about the state of the place," he said. "I haven't managed to do much since I heard."

Daisy closed the pizza box and sat down at the kitchen table. "Douglas," she said gently. "What was Mel doing at my salon last night?"

He blinked at her vacantly. "I don't know. She was meant to be at a friend's book launch at the library."

Daisy frowned. Clayton hadn't said a word about a book launch. If the library had been open for a function last night, Clayton would have been there.

"Did she say who the friend was?"

"No." He poured water into both mugs, then got the milk out of the fridge. "You know what she's like, always out and about with someone or another. Although she's usually home for dinner."

He put the two mugs on the table and sat down. Daisy got up and calmly took two tea bags out of the tin by the kettle and popped them into the cups. Douglas didn't even notice. She added a spoonful of sugar to his and gave it a stir.

"Is there anyone you can stay with for a bit?" she asked gently. He wasn't in a good way, Melanie's death had hit him very hard. "Or anyone you can call to come over?"

He dropped his head, and Daisy saw a tear roll down his face. It was clear he'd loved his wife. "I have a sister in Kent."

"Why don't you call her?" suggested Daisy, taking out her phone. "Would you like me to do it?"

He didn't reply. Daisy bit her lip. "Do you have her number?"

"It's in the phone book by the telephone stand in the hall," he said.

Daisy got up and went into the hall. In the console drawer under the telephone was a well-used address book. Obviously, Douglas hadn't entered the digital age yet. Did he even have a mobile phone? She brought it back to the kitchen.

"What's her name?"

"Iris." His voice was a low mumble.

Daisy looked up the number and gave Iris a ring. The call lasted less than a minute. She gave Iris the news, and his sister, who sounded like a capable, take-charge kind of woman, said she'd drive through immediately. Daisy relayed the message to Douglas, who merely nodded. Daisy felt better knowing there was someone coming who would take care of him.

There was a knock on the door. Firm, three knocks. The police.

Daisy went to answer it and smiled at the look of surprise on DCI McGuinness's face. "Hello again, Detective."

"Daisy. What are you doing here?"

"Paying my condolences." She stood back to let him enter. Sergeant Buckley followed close behind. "Douglas is not in a good way, so be gentle with him."

McGuinness turned. "I hope you're not involving yourself in my investigation."

"I told you, I'm paying my respects. And just so you know, I've called his sister. She's on her way over from Kent."

The detective frowned and walked ahead of her into the kitchen. Douglas was staring into his untouched cup of tea with the tea bag floating on the top.

"Mr. Haverstock. I'm Detective Chief Inspector McGuinness, and this is Sergeant Buckley. May we have a word?"

Douglas glanced up, nodded, then went back to staring into his teacup.

Daisy met the detective's gaze. "He's taken it rather badly."

McGuinness nodded, then took a seat. Daisy began loading the plates into the dishwasher.

"Can you tell us your wife's movements last night?"

Douglas grimaced. "Again?"

Daisy dropped the knives and forks into the cutlery section of the dishwasher, making as much noise as possible. McGuinness's voice was edgy. "Yes, if you don't mind."

"She went to a friend's book launch at the library."

"Do you know which friend?"

"No, I don't. She didn't say, okay? She never told me where she was going, she was very independent that way. She liked to go out, I didn't, so she usually went out without me. That was the way we were. It didn't mean I didn't love her."

He collapsed onto the table, sobbing. Daisy glanced up in alarm.

Both male detectives stared at him, unsure what to do.

Daisy flashed McGuinness a stern look and put her arm around the distraught husband.

"There, there, Douglas. It's okay. Here, have some tea." She grabbed a teaspoon and removed the tea bag. "It'll help with the shock."

He swiped at his eyes, then wrapped his fingers around the mug. "She did love me, you know. In her own way."

Daisy patted his shoulder. "I know."

"What are you doing questioning my suspect?" hissed DCI McGuinness once they'd left Douglas's house. His body was taut, and his eyes burned into hers.

"I wasn't questioning him," she retorted. "I merely asked him if Melanie had come back to the salon to look for me."

"And had she?" He exhaled heavily, hands on his hips, making a conscious effort to calm down.

"No, apparently not. He had no idea what she was doing there."

McGuinness turned away and began to pace up and down the pavement outside the house. Buckley stood beside the BMW, watching them.

"The man has no alibi for last night."

Daisy rolled her eyes. "Seriously? Did you see the state of him?"

"He could be acting."

"Him?" Daisy shook her head so her curls bounced. "He deals with figures all day. Lying and murder are a little out of his comfort zone."

McGuinness paused for a moment, then turned to his DS. "What do you think, Buckley?"

The sergeant flushed to the roots of his buzz cut. "I tend to agree with Miss Thorne, sir."

McGuinness grimaced. "Okay, we'll put him on ice for now. Do you have the sister's phone number, in case we need to get a hold of him?"

Daisy read it off her phone, and Buckley took it down.

"I'd like to speak to your stylist, Penny, about where she was last night, too."

Daisy sighed. "Penny went to a hen party. She left at eight and went home to shower and change before meeting the other girls at a pub in Esher. There is no way she killed Melanie."

"That may be the case, but I'd like to question her myself," McGuinness said. His look said not to argue.

Daisy sighed. "Suit yourself. She's at a wedding all day, so the best time to get her is tomorrow at the salon."

"Noted. Thank you. And now, if you'll kindly stay away from my suspects, I'll try to get on with the case."

Daisy put her hands on her hips. "Did it cross your mind that I'm also a victim here? Someone used my scissors to murder Melanie, putting me firmly at the top of your suspect list. If you don't find out who did this, I could go to jail."

"I'm well aware of that," he snapped. "Why do you think I'm trying so hard to catch the killer? Do you think I don't care about what happens to you?"

Daisy stared at him. He cared about her. A warm glow spread through her body, but before she had time to formulate a reply, he added, "You could give me some credit. I'm not entirely useless. I have been known to put the odd perpetrator behind bars."

"I was just trying to help," Daisy murmured. His reputation of late had been impressive. Even though she hadn't seen much of him, Krish, who had a mole in dispatch at the Guildford Police Station, had kept her informed.

He softened his tone. "Just because you helped me solve one crime, doesn't mean you have the right to get involved in this one."

"Even if it concerns me?"

"Especially if it concerns you," he said with an edge to his voice. "There's a killer on the loose who has framed you for a murder they committed. My advice is to keep your head down and stay out of trouble."

He had a point. But she couldn't just sit back and do nothing, not when her freedom, her reputation, her very existence was at stake. "All the more reason to catch this person, and quickly."

He shot her a stern look. "That is what I'm trying to do."

Daisy relented. He was under enough stress without having to worry about her. There were dark shadows beneath his eyes, and she knew he probably hadn't slept much last night, if at all. "Okay, I'll keep a low profile from now on."

McGuinness gave her a suspicious look. "I'll believe that when I see it."

He made to get in the car. "Oh, there's something you should know," Daisy called after him. He stopped and turned slowly on his heel.

"There wasn't a function at the library last night. Clayton, the head librarian, came into the salon just after five, and he didn't mention a book launch."

McGuinness gave her a hard stare. "Are you sure?"

"I'm certain, he would have mentioned it. He was going home to look after his mother, she's got dementia. You should obviously check with him, but that's what he told me."

McGuinness nodded. "Will do."

Daisy smiled. "Well, I'd best be on my way. It was nice seeing you again, Paul."

He didn't return her smile, but there was a softness in his gaze as he bid her farewell.

Chapter Seven

The salon was in an uproar when Daisy arrived at work on Monday morning. DCI McGuinness stood inside the front door with his trusty sidekick, his hulking presence and grim expression unnerving both the staff and the customers.

Krish was running around brandishing a hair dryer, his usually smooth mahogany face blotchy and flushed. For a moment, Daisy wondered whether he'd been electrocuted, then she realised he was just overexcited at the prospect of having the tall, handsome detective in the salon. Mrs. Brocklehurst was sitting unattended, half her hair in silver wrappers, while Lesley Grant lay with her head in a basin.

Penny hovered behind the reception desk, as white as the pages of the appointment book in front of her, looking like one of Niall Barclay's racehorses about to bolt, and Asa was nowhere to be seen.

"Good morning, Inspector, Sergeant." Daisy brushed past the two policemen to confront Krish.

"What on earth is going on?" she demanded, tossing her handbag on a vacant chair.

"The chief inspector wants to interview us," said Krish, his eyes slightly glazed.

"Okay, so why are you running around like a crazy person?"

I'm trying to reorganise everyone. He wants to talk to Asa first, but she won't come out from behind the wash-basins. She's terrified of coppers, he mouthed.

"One moment, Lesley," Daisy called to the woman with sopping wet hair, then went behind the basins to find Asa.

The normally lippy black girl was crouching on the floor, holding the hose in front of her like a weapon. Luckily, it wasn't on or water would be gushing all over the floor.

"Follow me, Asa," ordered Daisy, then marched into the kitchenette.

Asa scrambled to her feet and darted inside behind her.

"I can't go out there, Daisy," she said, her eyes huge. "I don't like them coppers."

"DCI McGuinness has a job to do. We have to cooperate."

"But I don't trust 'em. Talking to coppers never did anyone any good. You ask my uncle Sol. He was arrested for having a spliff in his pocket. He told them it was medicinal, but they didn't believe 'im."

"Do you have any drugs on you, Asa?"

She shook her head. "I don't smoke, you know dat."

"Then you have nothing to worry about. DCI McGuinness just wants to ask you a few questions about Saturday afternoon."

"What if he arrests me for killin' Melanie Whatshername?" Her lower lip quivered.

Daisy sighed. The girl was quite hysterical. "He just wants to ask you what time you left work, and where you went, that's all."

Asa eyed her suspiciously. "How'd you know that's all he wants?"

"Because then he can eliminate you from his enquiries."

There was a pause as Asa turned and glanced at the two policemen. She reminded Daisy of a frightened hare eyeing out a salivating hound. "Look, would it help if I sat with you?" she asked.

Asa gave a slow nod.

"Okay, come on. Let's get this over with. Then things can get back to normal," she muttered.

She beckoned to McGuinness. "Do you want to come into the kitchen? We'll do the interviews here. There's not much space, but it's better than alarming the customers."

McGuinness nodded and strode across the salon. He wore a grey shirt under a black suit, with a maroon tie. He looked smart and capable. The rings under his stormy-grey eyes had faded a bit.

Daisy told Asa to bring in four chairs, then she instructed Penny to finish washing Lesley's hair. Krish had already gone back to Mrs. Brocklehurst's highlights, although he kept casting excited glances at Paul.

The whole village would soon know the police were in her salon questioning her staff. Krish was the worst gossip in Edgemead. He was also a font of local knowledge, but right now, Daisy wasn't sure the latter outweighed the former. If the public thought one of her employees, or even worse, *she* was a murderer, she could kiss her business goodbye.

Asa trembled in the corner, holes in her skin tight jeans, twisting her olive-green jumper into knots in front of her. Daisy sat down next to her.

DCI McGuinness lowered his large frame onto one of the remaining chairs, while Buckley closed the door. He didn't sit down, as it was rather crowded in the tiny kitchen.

Daisy thought about offering tea, but she didn't want to prolong Asa's agony. Best get this over with as quickly as possible.

"Asa, what is your full name?" asked McGuinness.

She swallowed and said, "Asavella Gordon-Smith."

He raised his eyebrow at the double-barrel.

"My mama wanted to keep her own name when she married my father, so they combined the two."

He nodded. "How old are you, Asa?"

"Twenty-three." Her lower lip stuck out in a sulk.

"Okay. Can you tell me your movements on Saturday afternoon?"

Asa glanced at Daisy, who nodded reassuringly. "Well, I was here, wasn't I?" she said.

"Until what time?" asked McGuinness with more patience than Daisy thought possible.

"Till five. That's when I knock off."

"And then where did you go?"

Asa fidgeted in her seat. "I went to Camden with my mates. Jazzy James was playing at the Funk House. He's banging."

McGuinness didn't react, but Buckley looked dubious.

"Did you go straight there after work?" the detective asked.

"Yeah. I said I did, didn't I?"

"And your friends will vouch for you?"

"Of course they will. You going to call them and check up on me?"

"My sergeant will do that, if you'll give him their contact details once we're done here."

She didn't reply, although her bottom lip protruded more than ever. Buckley made a note.

McGuinness leaned back in his chair. "Thank you, Asa, you can go now." The young woman shot out of the room almost before Buckley could open the door.

Daisy sighed. "Sorry about that. I've never seen her so edgy before."

McGuinness almost smiled. "That's okay. We're used to it. Could I speak to Krish next?"

"That's me," sang Daisy's head stylist, who'd been hovering outside the door. He gave Buckley the once-over, then sat cross-legged on Asa's vacant chair and flashed his big brown eyes at McGuinness. "Fire away, Detective."

"I'll leave you to it," said Daisy, hiding a smile. She almost thought McGuinness was going to call her back.

"I'm scared, Daisy," moaned Penny, as Daisy reappeared by her side. She was cutting Lesley's hair, while Mrs. Brocklehurst was safely under the dryer waiting for her highlights to set. "What if they don't believe me?"

"Don't worry." Daisy squeezed her arm. "It'll be fine. This is just a preliminary questioning, that's all. They're asking everyone the same questions. Besides, I'm their prime suspect, not you."

Lesley gasped.

"Don't worry," said Daisy quickly. "None of us had anything to do with Melanie's death."

"I hope not," Lesley replied, her gaze flitting to the scissors in Penny's hand.

Daisy gritted her teeth. The day had not gotten off to a very good start.

Her next customer arrived, so she didn't notice Krish come out of the kitchenette and Penny go in. It was only when a pink-faced Krish dashed over some time later that Daisy realised something was wrong.

"Penny's in tears," he hissed. "McGuinness really laid into her."

"Oh no," breathed Daisy, putting down the hair dryer. Mrs. Connolly's cut and blow-dry would have to wait. She knocked on the kitchen door, only to have Sergeant Buckley open it.

"Can I come in?" she asked.

"I'd rather you didn't," said McGuinness, frowning.

Daisy peered past Buckley at Penny, who sat quaking in the corner. She was the colour of a sheet.

"What have you done to her?" she demanded, storming across the room and giving Penny a hug. The redhead collapsed onto her shoulder, tears pouring down her face. "Oh, Daisy, they think I killed Melanie."

Daisy glared at McGuinness. "What motive does she have, Inspector?"

He looked chagrined. "We haven't established that yet."

"She doesn't have one, that's why," Daisy snapped, pulling Penny to her feet. "Unless you're going to arrest her, this interview is over."

She led Penny from the kitchenette and plonked her

down on the sofa by the front door. "I'll make some tea," she told her, "just as soon as I get rid of those two."

Penny sniffed and nodded.

"You are a bully, Paul," she told McGuinness, waving her finger in his face. Buckley's eyes widened. He'd clearly never seen anyone talk to his boss like that before. "Penny had nothing to do with this. She didn't even know the victim."

"She has no alibi for the night of the murder," he told her. "And when we questioned her about her whereabouts, she fell apart. She couldn't account for the time between leaving the salon and getting to the pub in Esher."

"She's terrified," hissed Daisy. "Is this how you get convictions? You frighten your suspects into submission?"

"Only if they're guilty," he retaliated.

"Well, she's not."

McGuinness stared at her for a long moment, then said, "We are going to have to talk to her again. She arrived at the pub after nine o'clock, and she left here at eight. It doesn't take an hour to drive to Esher."

"No, but it does to go home, shower, blow-dry your hair, get dressed, put on makeup, and then drive to Esher," Daisy pointed out, annoyed with him. "She was meeting Niall Barclay later that night, so she wanted to look her best."

"Except she didn't meet him, did she?" McGuinness corrected. "Something about a mare giving birth?"

"Why don't you call him and check?" snapped Daisy, who'd had enough of his pestering her staff. "He owns a massive stud farm near Cobham. You'll fit right in. Now, if you don't mind, I have customers to attend to."

He made to leave through the salon, but she put her

hand on his chest. "This way, please. You've done enough damage to my business already today."

She opened the back door. The forensics tent had disappeared, and the alleyway showed no sign of the incident that had occurred only two nights ago.

Buckley left first, tightening his jacket around him, but Paul lingered. "I didn't mean to cause any trouble for you," he said, pausing on the step.

"Yes, you did," she retorted. "Otherwise you wouldn't have been so hard on Penny. Next time save the strong-arm tactics for when you've actually arrested someone."

Daisy closed the door in his face.

Chapter Eight

"Bravo," said Krish, clapping.

Daisy turned around, her face burning. How dare Paul waltz into her place of work and terrorise her staff? Who did he think he was?

"That man is so annoying," she fumed, smacking the kettle on.

He grinned. "Tell me about it."

Daisy glanced at him. "You say that like it's a good thing."

"He is rather macho, isn't he? That whole steely-eyed detective thing he's got going on . . . It's so attractive."

"You're impossible," she told him, taking four mugs out of the cabinet and placing them on the counter next to the kettle.

"He definitely has a soft spot for you."

Daisy scowled at him. "Now you're being ridiculous."

He shrugged. "Not many people could tell him off like that and get away with it, mark my words."

"He was out of line," Daisy snapped. "Poor Penny's in a terrible state. Someone had to bring him down a few notches."

"Well, you certainly did that." He giggled.

Daisy sighed. "Why don't you make yourself useful and go and comfort Penny."

"Yes, boss," he said and scampered off.

Daisy made her senior stylist a cup of sweet tea—she seemed to be doing that a lot lately—and went to sit with her on the couch. Penny's eyes were bloodshot, and her nose was red, but even this couldn't dim her innate beauty. Her high cheekbones glistened with tears, and her full lips were scarlet from gnawing on them. Even her smudged black eyeliner enhanced the iridescent green of her irises.

"He got me so flustered"—she blew her nose on a piece of toilet paper—"that I didn't know what I was saying. He barked so many questions at me, I couldn't keep up. Did I go straight home? Did I get dressed or do my makeup first? How did I wear my hair? Why didn't I meet Niall? Honestly, what does all that matter?"

"It's okay." Daisy handed her the tea. "He has a knack for rattling people. He seems to think it's effective detective work."

"Works for me," murmured Krish, taking out Mrs. Brocklehurst's foils.

"Shut up, Krish," snapped Daisy, then turned to Penny. "Why don't you take a long lunch break and pull yourself together. Do something to take your mind off all this. Yvette's, next door, is having a sale. I saw some great autumn jackets in the window. Go on, we're not that busy today. We can spare you for a couple of hours."

"Thanks, Daisy." Penny's lower lip trembled. She looked like she was about to burst into tears again.

After Penny had left, Daisy cleared up a little. What a shambles. The police obviously had nothing to go on if they were still sniffing around her and her staff. Her thoughts drifted back to Saturday evening and settled on Liz Roberts, her last customer of the day. Had she really left when she'd said she had? She'd called the Uber from the salon, but Daisy hadn't heard her specify a time. But then, she hadn't been paying attention to the call. What if Liz had lied and snuck around the back to murder Melanie? The timing fit.

Then she sighed. How would Liz have known Melanie was going to be there? Unless they'd planned to meet beforehand. But why here?

She grabbed the broom and swept the floor even though there wasn't any hair on it. It helped her think. She was missing something . . . What was Mel doing back here that night? That's what she needed to find out.

Speak of the devil, Daisy thought, as the front door tinkled and the sturdy figure of the head of the Edgemead Women's Institute swept in. She wore a high-neck black poncho that swished around her like a cape. Her face was flushed, her eyes glistened, and Daisy had never seen her looking so animated.

"Is it true?" Liz Roberts demanded, getting straight to the point.

"Is what true?" asked Daisy calmly, even though she knew perfectly well what Liz was referring to.

"Melanie Haverstock. Is it true that she was killed outside your salon?"

Daisy grimaced. Bad news travelled fast.

"Yes, it's true," she said, wishing it wasn't. They'd already had one cancellation this afternoon. Her customer had given a flimsy excuse about coming down with a cold, but Daisy could hear she was lying.

"Good heavens," Liz breathed, her chest heaving. There was a thin layer of sheen on her forehead and perspiration droplets on her upper lip. Good heavens, had she run all the way here from her house? It was three-quarters of a mile away. Liz never drove into town. She considered it lazy and wasteful. "Besides, the exercise is good for me," she was fond of telling people. At least she practised what she preached.

"Did you find her body?" she asked.

Daisy nodded. She didn't want to relive that moment, thank you very much. It had taken her ages to fall asleep on Saturday night after the taxi had dropped her off at home, images of Melanie's dead body lying facedown in the rain swirling around in her mind.

"I can't believe it," went on Liz, clutching her bag to her chest. "I really can't believe it. She's really dead."

"Why not?" asked Daisy, giving Liz a skew look. Her cheeks were flushed, and her eyes shone. If anything, she seemed overjoyed by the news, like she'd won the lottery. "Why can't you believe she's dead?"

"Oh, it's just so bizarre. Nothing like this ever happens in Edgemead," Liz said quickly while she tried to compose herself. Daisy wasn't buying it. "I was having tea with one of the WI ladies and she told me. I was so surprised that I had to come down here and find out for myself whether it was true."

"Yes, I'm afraid it is. Melanie was stabbed in the back." She left out the bit about her scissors being the murder weapon. It wouldn't be long before everyone was talking about it, but it wouldn't be because of her.

"Amazing," said Liz, her face lighting up again. "Do they know who did it?"

"No, not yet," said Daisy. She could see Krish placing the dryer over his customer's head, straining to hear every word.

"Well, someone must have hated her very much to do that to her," Liz said, almost gleefully.

"Yes, I suppose so." Daisy touched Liz's arm, concerned. "Are you alright, Liz? You seem a bit out of sorts."

"Oh, I'm perfectly fine, Daisy," she said. "In fact, I've never been better." She did look remarkably well, considering the subject matter.

"I take it you found a substitute speaker for your next meeting?" Daisy asked, recalling how distraught Liz had been on Saturday. Was it really the speaker pulling out of the meeting that had gotten her so worked up? Or was it something more? Something to do with Melanie, perhaps?

"Oh yes, thanks to you. I phoned your friend, and she's going to show us how to make Christmas cards. It'll be a hoot."

"Melanie was your treasurer, wasn't she?" Daisy mused. "You must have known her fairly well."

"Oh, we weren't friends," she snapped, her demeanour suddenly changing. The sparkle disappeared, and her lips flattened into a thin line.

Daisy scarcely covered her surprise.

Liz crinkled her nose like she'd smelled something bad. "She did the books for the Institute, but that's all. We didn't see eye to eye."

"Did you have a falling-out?" asked Daisy, curious now. Melanie had a tendency to rub people up the wrong way.

Liz hesitated. "Something like that. It was over how the funds were allocated, you see. We had very different ideas for the future of the WI."

"I see." Something wasn't right here, but Daisy couldn't put her finger on it. Liz Roberts was acting very strangely.

"Did you get home okay the other night?" Daisy asked her, purposely changing the subject. Liz blinked, confused by the sudden shift in topic.

"You know, in the rain. I hope you didn't ruin your hair?"

Liz registered, and gave a little laugh. "Oh no. I called the Uber, remember?" She patted her hair. "Still intact."

"I'm glad."

"Well, it was lovely talking to you, Daisy dear, but I have to dash. I've got an appointment on the other side of town. Ta-ta." And she pirouetted out of the salon into the high street.

"Well, I'll be . . ." Daisy muttered, staring after her.

Krish came over. "Was it my imagination, or did she look happy that Melanie was dead?"

Daisy shook her head. "I don't understand it. I could have sworn she was smiling. That's very out of character for Liz. She's usually the pinnacle of decorum. I would have expected her to be planning the memorial service or arranging something in Melanie's honour."

"She's a strange one," declared Asa from the back. "I always thought there was something not quite right about her."

Daisy glanced at their only customer, who was safely tucked away under the industrial hair dryer. She wouldn't have heard a thing.

"That," she said slowly, "was very, very odd."

Chapter Nine

Daisy met her best friend, Floria, at a trendy new coffee shop in Edgemead called the Mug and Bean. It was fast becoming one of their favourite haunts. Warm and cosy, it smelled of coffee beans and pastries, and it was the perfect place to unwind after a hard day or warm up after a freezing cold one. Today fit both those descriptions. Daisy desperately needed to see a friendly face and indulge in a hot chocolate—not necessarily in that order.

Floria and her fiancé, Josh, were already there when she arrived.

"Over here!" Floria waved from across the room. They were sitting at a high table close to the window. Outside it had started drizzling, the rain pattering against the floor-to-ceiling windowpanes.

Daisy hurried over and embraced her friend. "Oh, it's so good to see you."

She kissed Josh on both cheeks. The two of them had been dating for over a year now, and Josh had recently moved into Floria's apartment in Chelsea. She couldn't be happier for her best friend. Josh was warm, funny, and steady enough to handle Floria *and* her family drama. It took a special kind of guy to deal with Floria's opera diva mother's highly publicised murder, her celebrity party-planning business (Sir Elton was a personal friend), her three famous half sisters, and her somewhat wild reputation, although to be fair, she had calmed down since she'd been with Josh. Secretly, Daisy thought the Aussie financier quite enjoyed Floria's impulsive streak, although he'd never admit it.

"Can I get you something, Daisy?" asked Josh, ever the gentleman. Originally from Sydney, he'd met Floria when he'd helped set up her party-planning company, Prima Donna Productions, last year, shortly after her infamous mother's death.

"Please. I'll have a large hot chocolate—with extra whipped cream," she said.

"That bad?" He grinned and headed to the bar.

"And sprinkles," Floria called after him, then she turned to Daisy and said in a hushed voice, "I heard all about it from Donna. Apparently, your handsome detective, McGuinness, called her to confirm her whereabouts on the night of the murder."

"Firstly, he's not *my* handsome detective," she huffed, still annoyed at him for the way he'd harangued her staff, "and secondly, I'm not surprised he called her. He's very thorough."

"Luckily she was performing Bartok's Violin Concerto No. 2 in front of three thousand people on Saturday night. Not even DCI McGuinness can argue with that."

Daisy didn't smile.

"My, you are in a bad way," said Floria, her easy smile replaced by a worried frown. She looked lovely in a vivid blue blouse that matched her eyes, and denim jeans that hugged her voluptuous, Marilyn Monroe figure. A fluffy, cream faux-fur coat lay over the back of her chair.

By comparison, Daisy felt washed out and exhausted. She leaned back into the comfy leather armchair and sighed. "Paul came to the salon this morning and frightened Penny and Asa half to death. Krish is smitten, and several customers have already cancelled their appointments for this week. I'm worried if this carries on, I'm going to lose business."

"Bloody hell," mumbled Floria, then she said thoughtfully, "Firstly, I don't think you'd ever lose business, you're far too well liked, and even if you or one of your staff were convicted of murder, you're still the only hairdresser in Edgemead, so you'd have to stay open. What would Ruth do without her morning blow-dry or the Fernwood ladies without their blue rinses?"

Daisy laughed. She could never stay down when Floria was around.

"And secondly," continued Floria. "Paul should know better. He's clearly barking up the wrong tree if he thinks you had anything to do with Melanie's murder. What's wrong with him?"

"All the evidence points to me," Daisy reminded her. "But it's the bad press that worries me. What if more customers cancel?" She had bills to pay, and renting property right on the high street wasn't cheap. The foot traffic it brought in made up for it, but if sales dropped off, she'd be in real trouble.

"It won't come to that," Floria said, squeezing her hand. "You're innocent, and when they find the real killer, all this will blow over. In fact, you'll probably have customers queuing up outside the salon, eager to find out the real story. You know what this village is like."

Daisy did. When Floria's mother, the famous opera diva, Dame Serena Levanté, had been murdered, Floria and her three half sisters—Donna, Mimi, and Carmen—had come under intense scrutiny from the police as well as the local and international press. It had taken months before the hoo-ha had died down. Even Daisy had had paparazzi camping outside her cottage once it became known she'd had a hand in solving the murder.

"What's worse is that neither Penny nor I have an alibi for Saturday night. I was at the salon locking up, while Penny was on her way to a bachelorette party in Esher, but there's at least half an hour when we were both alone and unaccounted for."

"Paul must know that neither you nor Penny are capable of something like this?" said Floria, as Josh came back with the hot chocolate and another espresso for himself. Floria was nursing a latte.

"Thanks, Josh." Daisy took a sip, closing her eyes in ecstasy. "That is so good." Then, she looked at her friend. "Unfortunately, it doesn't matter what he thinks, he's still got to do his job, and the evidence says it was my scissors that killed her. Did I tell you he dragged me down to the Guildford Police Station and interviewed me under caution on Saturday night?"

"No." Floria looked shocked.

Josh frowned. "Is he allowed to do that?"

"Apparently so. I volunteered to help with his enquiries." Daisy gave a wry grin. "What else could I do? I did find the body."

"You could get legal representation," suggested Josh.

"Maybe you should, Dais," said Floria, glancing worriedly at her fiancé and then back at Daisy. "This could be serious."

"Don't I know it." For a moment Daisy wished she could sink into the chair and disappear.

"Greg will know someone," Josh said, mentioning Donna's husband, who was a trust attorney. He'd handled Dame Serena's estate, which was how he'd met Floria's sister.

"Maybe I'll give him a ring." Daisy felt the pressure bearing down on her. "If only I could figure out who stole my cutting scissors, then I'd have a better idea of who killed Mel."

"Are you thinking of launching your own investigation?" Floria asked, her brows rising.

Daisy hesitated. "I think I'm going to have to, otherwise I'm the prime suspect."

Josh looked grim. "Should you be getting involved, with a killer out there?"

"I'm already involved." She sighed. "I appreciate your concern, Josh, but someone tried to frame me when they used my scissors to stab Melanie. It had to be one of my customers, which makes me the best placed to get to the bottom of this."

"She does have a point," murmured Floria.

Josh frowned. "Just be careful, Daisy. And if you need anything, all you have to do is call."

"Thanks, Josh." She squeezed his hand.

"Did you know her well?" asked Floria. "Melanie, I mean."

"Sort of." Daisy blew on the hot drink to cool it. "We were at school together, but she wasn't very nice back then. We certainly weren't friends."

"Really? I can't imagine you not being friends with anyone."

Daisy grimaced. "It wasn't my fault we weren't friends. Something happened, and I couldn't quite forgive her after that."

"Now I am intrigued," said Floria, getting comfortable. "Do tell."

Daisy took a breath. "When I was sixteen, I had this boyfriend called David. He lived in our street. I remember he played for the local football club, and we used to go and watch the matches on weekends. He was tall and athletic with longish hair and mischievous blue eyes. It was those eyes that attracted me to him in the first place. All the girls were into him, so I couldn't believe it when he asked me out."

"What happened?" asked Floria, twisting her coffee mug round and round.

"We dated for about six months, and I was on cloud nine. I remember thinking this can't be true, how can David Mornington be my boyfriend?" She smiled at the memory. "I was young, and he was my first real boyfriend."

"Ah, the sweet innocence of youth," sighed Floria.

"It turns out it was too good to be true," Daisy said with a dry laugh. "Not long after that, I caught them making out under the grandstand. I was devastated. I remember crying into my pillow over him." She shook her head at the memory. "It seems silly now, but at the time it was very hurtful, and Melanie rubbed my nose in it for weeks, parading him in front of me at football matches and any other chance she got."

"What a bitch," gasped Floria, her colour up.

"Yes, she was a bit of a bully, actually. Always taking other people's boyfriends like it was a game. I don't think she even liked them, you know. She did it because she could. It made her feel good about herself in a sad way."

Josh put his hand on Floria's leg. "It takes two to tango."

"Yes, quite," said Daisy. "David wasn't blameless, but then he was a teenage boy and she had the biggest boobs in the year group."

Josh laughed.

"Anyway," Daisy continued, "things were pretty tense after that. I didn't have much to do with her, and once school ended, we lost touch. She went to university in Bristol, I believe. It was years later when I saw her again."

"She came back to Edgemead?" asked Josh. He hadn't lost his Australian twang despite having lived in the U.K. for over a decade.

"Yes, one day she waltzed into Ooh La La and booked an appointment. She acted as if nothing had happened, like we were two old mates who hadn't seen each other in a while."

"And you were okay with that?" asked Floria, tilting her head to the side.

Daisy shrugged. "I didn't see the point in dredging up old wounds. It was so long ago, and I can barely remember the guy. Goodness knows what became of him."

"I don't know any David Mornington in the Premier League," scoffed Josh. "So, I don't think his football career panned out."

Daisy chuckled.

Floria pursed her lips. "Probably wise. You're a much bigger person than me, Dais. I'd have given her a piece of my mind, even all these years later."

"Except now she's dead," said Josh. "And someone killed her with your scissors, putting you directly in the line of fire."

Daisy bit her lip. That was the gist of it. "Yep."

They fell silent, all three thinking about the repercussions of what had happened.

"Perhaps you weren't the only person Melanie upset," suggested Floria. "It sounds like she was a piece of work. I didn't know her personally, but I've seen her flitting around town in those ridiculously short skirts and high heels. Totally inappropriate for a woman her age."

"She was thirty-two," said Daisy.

"Exactly," sniffed Floria. "No one over the age of eighteen should wear miniskirts that short. If she bent over, there wouldn't be much left to the imagination."

Josh laughed. "Maybe that was the idea."

"She did have a hot body," Daisy pointed out.

"Her breasts were fake," said Floria, determined not to acknowledge any redeeming features. "But my point is that she obviously pissed someone off enough to kill her."

"That's quite possible," said Josh, regarding them both over the top of his espresso. "But if I were you, I'd keep this story about the footballer boyfriend to yourself. It does give you a motive."

Floria smacked him on the thigh. "Josh! How can you say that?"

"I'm just throwing it out there," he said. "That's what the police will think if it ever comes out."

"Seriously? That I killed her because she stole my boyfriend in secondary school?"

Josh shrugged. "Be that as it may, you need to be careful, Daisy. If someone is trying to frame you, you might be in danger."

"Oh gosh, Dais," gasped Floria, going white. "I hadn't thought of that. Maybe you should come and stay with me until this is over. I can move to Brompton Court for a few weeks, it's no problem. Josh won't mind, will you darling?"

Brompton Court was Floria's family home, a gorgeous Georgian stone mansion with acres of ground, including a lake and woods, situated between the small village of Edgemead and the larger town of Esher. Floria had inherited it after her mother's untimely death.

"No, and it might be for the best," agreed Josh. "You'll be safe there with Floria, and I believe Violeta and Pepe still live on the property." He was referring to the late Dame Serena's housekeeper and her husband, who worked as the groundsman on the estate. They'd elected to stay on after Serena's death to oversee the place now that it was empty.

Daisy hesitated. As much as she loved Brompton Court, it would make getting to work more difficult as she'd have to drive, which meant sitting in traffic for a good twenty minutes every morning and evening. From her cottage, it was less than a mile's walk across the meadow to the high street where the salon was located.

"Thanks, Floria," she said, deciding against it. "If I feel in any danger, I'll definitely take you up on it, but right now, it's more convenient if I stay where I am. Besides, if the killer is trying to frame me for the murder, they won't want to bump me off, will they? That would defeat the purpose."

Floria shivered. "Don't talk like that. It makes me nervous."

Josh took Floria's hand and rubbed it between both of his. "Seriously, Daisy, be careful."

She glanced at their intertwined hands and felt a wistful pang in her chest. For a moment, she wished she had someone who cared about her like that, someone whom she could turn to when she was anxious, hold when she was frightened. Her thoughts turned to Paul, and she visualised his large, ungainly hands wrapped around hers. No, she couldn't picture him doing that. Besides, he was more likely to be fastening handcuffs around her wrists, the way things were going. She drained the last of her hot chocolate. "Don't worry, I will."

"Anyone for a cookie?" asked Josh.

Daisy stood up. "That sounds great, I'm quite hungry. I'll get it."

She bought a plate of delicious, oozing chocolate-chip cookies. On the way back to the table, a feminine voice with a soft French accent said, " 'Allo Daisy."

Daisy halted. Yvette, the owner of the French boutique next door to Ooh La La, was sitting at a table in the corner working on her laptop. There was a large cappuccino in front of her and a half-eaten baguette. "Oh, hello, Yvette. I didn't see you sitting there. How are you?"

Yvette shrugged. "I'm okay. I was sorry to hear about what 'appened outside your salon the other night."

"Thank you. Yes, it was quite a shock."

Then it hit her. Yvette had come into the salon the day of the murder too, but to cancel an appointment, not to make one. It had completely slipped Daisy's mind. What time was that? Eleven o'clock? Twelve?

She was just about to ask when Yvette's phone rang. The elegant Frenchwoman held up a perfectly manicured finger and answered the call. Daisy gave her a parting smile and retreated to her table.

"I've just remembered something," she said excitedly, putting the biscuits down. "Yvette Bechard was also in the salon on Saturday morning. I'd completely forgotten until I saw her sitting there."

"Yvette, who owns the French clothing store next door to you?" Floria asked.

Daisy nodded.

"I quite like her stuff. She has a beautiful collection of French scarves, and I think I bought a hat there once for Ascot." Floria twisted around to catch a glimpse of Yvette, but the Frenchwoman was tucked behind a wall, out of sight. Only her patent-leather pumps were visible beneath the table.

"Yes, she came in to cancel her appointment. I thought it was strange at the time, she has a monthly standing appointment to cover her grey." Daisy dropped her voice. "She's older than she looks."

"Aren't we all?" Floria grinned.

Daisy narrowed her eyes. "I think she might be having money troubles."

"That's a shame," murmured Floria. "So many high street stores are going under these days."

"Just because she's in financial trouble, doesn't mean she killed Melanie," Josh pointed out reasonably.

"No, it doesn't," sighed Daisy. "They knew each other, I think, but I'm not sure how well. Melanie didn't have a lot of friends in the village."

"I can't imagine why," muttered Floria, rolling her eyes. "I wouldn't let her anywhere near my man." She squeezed Josh's leg.

Judging by the besotted look Josh gave her, Daisy didn't think Floria had anything to worry about. "My point is, she could have stolen the cutting scissors."

Both Josh and Floria stared at her.

"Do you think there's a possibility she is the killer?" Floria whispered.

Josh frowned and glanced repeatedly at Yvette's legs under the table, which was the only part of her they could see.

"I'm not saying that," reasoned Daisy. She mustn't jump to conclusions. "But she was in the salon around the time my scissors went missing, which makes her a suspect, so I can't discount her. Not yet."

"Shouldn't you mention this to Paul?" Floria's blue eyes clouded with concern. "I understand you wanting to get to the bottom of this, but it is his job to question the suspects, not yours."

"I will," Daisy reassured her, just as soon as she'd spoken to Yvette herself. First thing tomorrow morning.

Chapter Ten

Daisy waited until Yvette opened the store the next morning, then popped in on the pretense of checking out the sale. The French store owner was on the phone when she walked in, so Daisy threw her a friendly wave and proceeded to browse around the store. It was about the same size as the salon, but the walls were lined with pine shelving units and cabinets to showcase the merchandise. An old-fashioned French cash register sat on the counter-top beside a copy of *Le Monde* that Daisy knew the newsagent down the road ordered especially for her. On the other side of the counter stood an enormous vase of St. Joseph's Lilies.

Daisy perused the store, admiring and feeling the different textures and fabrics. Floria was right, there was an amazing selection of scarves. Not only did she stock the top designers like Hermes and Chanel, but she also had some very pretty high-street French brands in an assortment of colours and styles.

"*Non*," hissed Yvette down the line. "I told you before, I am not interested."

Daisy shifted closer to the till, pretending to admire an unusual peach hat with a cluster of feathers sticking out of it and a gauzy veil.

"Leave me alone." Yvette kept her voice low, but Daisy didn't miss the brittle edge and the way she clutched the countertop, her knuckles white.

Daisy moved away again as soon as Yvette hung up but watched her reflection in the store window. Yvette was fighting to control her emotions. She was usually so proud and independent, and Daisy was startled by the fear and vulnerability on the Frenchwoman's face.

She browsed some more, and eventually picked out a burnished orange silk scarf shot through with strands of copper, which she thought would go nicely with an outfit she had at home. Approaching the counter, she handed it to Yvette. "I'll take this one, please."

Yvette nodded, not trusting herself to speak. Her face was composed, but her hand shook as she scanned the scarf and put it into a plastic bag.

"Is everything alright, Yvette?" Daisy asked, softly.

"Yes, of course. Why wouldn't it be?" Yvette's chin went up a notch. Always elegant, always perfectly made up, the Frenchwoman had never shown any sign of weakness, until now.

Daisy nodded to the phone. "You sounded upset, that's all."

The store owner wrinkled her nose in disgust. "*That* was nothing."

Daisy nodded, desperate to find out what was upsetting Yvette, but reluctant to appear as if she were prying. "Well, if you ever need to talk, you know where I am."

Yvette glanced away.

It was worth a shot, thought Daisy. She took her debit card out of her purse and held it in front of the contactless payment machine. The transaction went through with a high-pitched beep.

"Thank you." Daisy smiled, taking the bag from Yvette. The Frenchwoman still wouldn't meet her gaze.

"See you soon," called Daisy as she left the store.

"Someone is harassing Yvette Bechard," Daisy informed Krish, Penny, and Asa when she got back to the salon. She'd stopped at Starbucks on the way and was juggling four caramel lattes, one with soy milk for Penny, and one with an extra shot, for Krish. She told them about the phone conversation and Yvette's shaken reaction.

"Do you think they want money from her?" Krish scratched his chin.

"Maybe she's in debt," suggested Penny.

"She might have a gambling problem," said Asa, who was setting up the nail bar, which was situated in the back corner of the salon beside the basins. It was only open in the mornings, but it was proving extremely popular, especially since Halloween was just around the corner. "Maybe she owes them loan sharks money and if she doesn't pay up, they'll smash her kneecaps."

"You watch too much TV," scoffed Krish.

"I don't think Yvette's the gambling type," mused Daisy, putting her bag down and glancing at the appointment book for the day. "It's more likely the business is in trouble and she's fighting foreclosure."

"That's awful," said Penny, mimicking Floria from the night before. "She has such lovely merchandise in there. I bought a stunning pink-sequined clutch-bag yesterday, when you gave me those few hours off."

"I just bought this." Daisy showed them her new scarf. "I love the colours."

"Very autumnal," remarked Krish, casting an approving eye over it. "It'll go well with your camel coat."

"Has Bianca called?" Daisy asked, realising for the first time that her new Polish assistant wasn't in yet. Bianca came in twice a week to help with the washing of customers' hair when Asa was busy with the nail bar. She was training her up to take over when Asa moved to the nail bar permanently.

"Not yet," said Krish.

She ran her finger down the page. They had a fairly busy day with some complicated colour jobs, a couple of perms, and a few heads of highlights, as well as several cut and blow-drys, but it was manageable.

Just then, the front door flew open, sending the bell into a frenzy of tinkles, and Bianca blew in, accompanied by a flurry of golden-brown leaves. She was a slip of a girl, about five foot four with dark hair and equally dark eyes in a narrow, earnest face, and she always seemed to be rushing around in a whirlwind. "Sorry I'm late."

Daisy knew she commuted from Surbiton, which was a good half hour away by train. "That's okay. Mrs. Benson's not here yet."

Thankfully, they had a slow start to the day. Their first customer was only due at ten o'clock—still five minutes to go.

Daisy was about to prepare the perm solution when the bell rang again and DCI McGuinness stalked in, bringing yet more leaves. He looked very smart in a dark, tailored winter coat, which he wore over his suit and tie.

"Hello, Detective," she said, trying not to notice how the silver tie brought out the grey specks in his eyes. "To what do we owe the honour?"

Krish dropped a ceramic hair-colouring bowl onto the floor with a clatter. Penny froze, comb in hand, and Asa slunk down her chair, trying to make herself as invisible as possible. Only Bianca stared openly at the tall, cloaked detective.

"Can I speak to you for a moment?" He ignored everyone else and gazed directly at her. Daisy wondered if he was aware of the havoc he created. "In private."

"Sure." She led the way into the kitchenette. "Shall I make some tea?"

"No, thank you. This isn't a social call."

No kidding. They hadn't had one of those in a long while. *More's the pity*, she thought, admiring the way his shoulders filled out the coat. There was a buzz, a vibrancy about him. Maybe he'd made some headway with the case. She could only hope.

"Can I see you after work today?" he asked.

Daisy glanced at him in surprise. "I take it that's not a social call, either?"

"Sorry." He gave a wry smile. "I need to talk to you about the case."

He needed to talk to her. Now, that sounded interesting.

"Sure," she said. "Where shall we meet? Do you want to grab something to eat?" Perhaps they could discuss it over a bottle of merlot and a pizza?

"Um, how about I come to you? Will six o'clock work?"

More and more intriguing. Last year, during the Serena Levanté investigation, he'd given her a lift home and
she'd invited him in for coffee, so he knew where she
lived.

"I'll be there." She smiled at him.

He nodded and opened the back door. "I won't disturb
your employees again," he said with a wry grin. "I know
how fond they are of me."

Chapter Eleven

The sun had already sunk by the time Daisy got home, and her little street was cast in murky shadows. She let herself into the cottage, picked up the post and put it on the countertop, then took her coat off and hung it on the hook behind the door. It was a little after six, which meant Paul would be there soon.

She checked her reflection in the mirror that hung in the living room behind the sofa and grimaced. Her hair was limp and stringy, and she had black mascara smudged underneath her eyes. Rummaging in her handbag, she located a comb and brushed her hair. Then she licked her fingertip and smoothed out the smudged mascara. There, that wasn't ideal, but it would have to do. She didn't have the time to redo her makeup. Then she frowned. Why would she, anyway? It was only DCI McGuinness coming round, and there was nothing between them. No reason to get glammed up.

She'd kicked off her shoes and put the kettle on when she heard Paul's BMW pull into her driveway. She waited until she heard his car door open and close, and the soft beep of his alarm, followed by his shoes on the porch before she opened the front door. A gust of frigid air swept in. It was going to rain again, probably tonight. She could smell it. "Hello again," she said with a smile.

He sort of returned the smile, then entered the living room. He seemed more distracted than he'd been that morning and a little more crumpled. His shirt wasn't quite so crisp, his tie was slightly askew, and worry lines were etched around his eyes.

"Tea?" Daisy asked him, taking his coat and hanging it on a series of hooks near the front door. It was warm from his body heat and smelled faintly of the woodsy aftershave he wore.

"Please." He walked into the room and hovered by the counter. "I'm sorry to intrude like this, but there are a couple of things I need to clear up."

"'Clear up'?" Daisy repeated. The kettle flicked off, and she poured the water into two teacups.

He hesitated, then glanced down at the pile of post on the countertop. "Who's Tim Watkins?" he asked.

"Ouch!" Daisy yelped as hot water sloshed onto her hand.

"You okay?"

"Yes, I'm fine." Except for the big red welt on her hand, which stung so badly it made her eyes water. "Tim was my fiancé. I still get some of his mail."

McGuinness stared at her. "Fiancé? I didn't realise you were engaged."

She ran her burned hand under the cold tap. No, she hadn't mentioned it before, with good reason, and she didn't really want to now, either. It was a long time ago and none of his business.

"It was a few years back," she said, keeping her tone light. "We lived together for a while before he . . ."

Disappeared.

"Before we broke up."

McGuinness fingered the envelope with the blue logo at the top. "You should notify the RSPCA that he no longer lives here."

"Yes, I know. I keep meaning to, but something always comes up." She placed a cup of tea in front of him.

"Thanks." He picked it up and moved into the living room, the unopened letters to her ex forgotten for the moment. "Shall we sit down?"

Daisy nodded and took her mug over to the sofa. McGuinness looked far too serious for her liking. She curled her legs up beneath her. "What did you want cleared up?" she asked.

He took a sip of his tea, then placed it on the glass coffee table. "It's to do with Melanie Haverstock and your relationship with her."

"My relationship with her?" Daisy fluttered her eyelashes at him. "We didn't have a relationship. I hardly knew her."

"That's not what I heard." His steel-grey eyes glided over her face, making her feel uncomfortable.

She frowned, her voice tight. "What did you hear?"

"I spoke to her mother this morning."

"Her mother?" Daisy was confused. She hadn't thought Melanie had any family left in Edgemead. If she did, she never mentioned them.

"Yes, she lives in Sunbury. She's widowed now. Her husband passed away several years ago."

"I didn't know." Daisy wondered where on earth he was going with this.

"Anyway"—McGuinness took a breath—"she told me you and Melanie have quite a colourful history, going back to your school days."

What could Melanie's aging mother possibly remember about her daughter's school friends, let alone Daisy, whom she'd never met?

"Well, I knew Melanie at school, but we weren't friends." Far from it.

"I believe there was an incident over a boyfriend. Is that right?"

Daisy stared at him. "An incident? No, of course not."

"She's lying?"

"Either that or she's confused. It was a long time ago." Daisy shook her head at him. "I've never met Melanie's mother. I'm surprised she even knows who I am."

"She remembers your name well. Melanie was quite cut up about the incident. She says you ruined her daughter's relationship. David, was it?"

She nodded, speechless. How was this even relevant?

"Well, apparently David was the love of her life, and they were going to get married."

Daisy, who had just taken a sip of tea, spluttered, "That is the most ridiculous thing I've ever heard. We were sixteen, for goodness' sake."

"So, it's not true?" His eyes seemed to burn right through her.

"No, it's not bloody true," she ranted. "In fact, the opposite is true." Heat and anger rose into her face. She broke off and took some deep breaths. How dare Melanie's mother say those things about her when it was *her* unprincipled daughter who . . . who'd . . . *Ugh.*

McGuinness waited for her to continue. When Daisy had calmed down, she said, "Let's get one thing straight. David was *my* boyfriend. We'd been together for about six months when *she* stole him from me." She blushed, feeling silly. How did any of this matter now? "One day I found them making out under the viewing benches on the football pitch." She still remembered the look of triumph on Melanie's face. She'd *wanted* Daisy to discover them. "I was shocked. It was the last thing I expected."

McGuinness continued to study her. "What then?"

She shrugged. "Then nothing. We broke up. He dated Melanie for a few months until she moved on to someone else. She did that quite frequently, by the way. I wasn't the only girl whose boyfriend she hijacked. It was a thing with her."

"They weren't serious?" he asked.

"Who? Mel and David? No way. A couple of months later, she was dating someone else. I don't know what her mother was on about."

David, the love of Melanie's life? Ha.

"What about you?" The question hung in the air.

Daisy glanced down at her teacup. "I decided not to date again until after I left school. It was less complicated that way." David's defection had hit her hard, not that she'd ever admit it, and her self-confidence had taken a knock. It hadn't improved much by the time she'd met Tim, her only serious relationship since school, and look how that turned out. Clearly, she didn't have very good taste in men.

"Probably wise," was all he said.

There was an awkward pause, then Daisy said, "Melanie's mother must have her wires crossed, or Melanie lied to her parents about the whole thing." It was more likely the latter.

McGuinness pursed his lips. "Yes, probably. Although, if it were true, it would give you a motive."

Daisy stood up. If he was going to insult her like this, he could leave. "It's not true. And even if it was, I don't see how something that happened fifteen years ago could have any bearing on this case. It's ancient history."

He stood up as well, towering over her. "That's why I came to speak to you," he said calmly. "To hear your side of the story."

"And whom do you believe?" She glared up at him.

"It doesn't matter whom I believe," he said, stubbornly.

Grr, she wanted to punch him. He was so annoyingly official. Couldn't he just be human, for once?

"It matters to me," she insisted.

He gazed at her for a long moment, then he said, "Off the record, of course I believe you, Daisy, but that doesn't make a stitch of difference."

"You don't have any evidence that I harmed Melanie Haverstock."

"Except the murder weapon, which has your prints all over it."

Okay, there was that.

"Other than that," she huffed.

"We haven't got the lab results back from your gloves or coat yet, but you have no alibi for the night of the murder, and now there looks to be motive. Technically, we have enough to bring you in."

At her angry stance, he raised his hands. "The prosecutor will twist that incident into a motive, no matter how long ago or inconsequential it was."

His stark expression worried her. This was turning into a nightmare. Despite being innocent, she may very well go down for this crime. And "murderess" wasn't a title she aspired to. It was time to redouble her efforts. She couldn't leave this in McGuinness's hands—she glanced down—no matter how capable they were. It was too risky—the odds were stacked against her. She had to figure out who had done this to Melanie before she herself was arrested.

"Have you spoken to any of the other suspects?" she asked. His time would be better served looking for the real killer rather than trying to disprove she'd done it.

"You know I can't discuss that with you."

She nodded. Typical. Ironic really, considering all his leads had come from her customer list.

McGuinness strode towards the door to fetch his coat. "I'm sorry it's not better news, Daisy," he said, back to his formal self. He lifted his coat down and put his long arms through the sleeves. "I'll let you know what we find with regards to the lab results."

"There won't be anything to find because I didn't touch the body." Then, she remembered about Yvette. "Oh, Paul."

He turned around, his hand poised on the doorknob. "This is where you tell me you've discovered something else, right?"

She couldn't quite muster a smile. "Something like that."

He let his hand drop. "Well, what is it?"

"There was another person who came into the salon on Saturday morning. Someone I forgot to tell you about."

"Oh?"

"Yvette Bechard. She works at the French boutique next door to Ooh La La, and she came in to cancel an appointment."

"Cancel an appointment?" His eyes narrowed.

"Yes, for next week."

"And you think she might have stolen the scissors?"

Daisy threw her hands in the air. "I don't know. I'm just telling you she was there, in the salon at about the time they went missing. I don't know whether she stole them or not. I wouldn't have thought she was the murdering type, but . . ."

"Right, I'll check her out. Thanks."

"There's something else."

He gave a half grin. "Of course there is."

Daisy ignored the sarcasm, she wasn't in the mood. "I'm not sure what's going on, but when I went into the boutique this morning, Yvette was in quite a state. She'd had an argument with someone over the phone. She had to tell whoever it was to leave her alone."

McGuinness gave her a hard look. "To leave her alone?"

"That's what she said. And she didn't sound happy about it. I got the impression she was being threatened."

He shook his head. "And you just remembered this now?"

"Actually, I remembered that she'd come into the salon last night when I bumped into her at the pub. I was there with Floria and Josh. It had completely slipped my mind until then. It was only this morning when I went to visit her that I overheard the threatening phone call."

He thought about this for a moment, then nodded. "Okay, I'll pay her a visit tomorrow, but Daisy . . ."

"Yes?"

"Don't go around questioning any more suspects. I appreciate the information, but leave that part to me. I'm on this."

"I didn't question her. I went into the store because she was having a sale, and I just happened to overhear her speaking on the telephone."

The corners of his lips turned up. "Sure you did."

Daisy pouted. "Has it occurred to you that all the leads you have in this case are thanks to me? It's my customers you're questioning, my scissors that were used, and my salon that was the scene of the crime. The least you could do is keep me informed."

He took a step closer to her. "Of course, but has it occurred to you that you are now the prime suspect in this investigation, so any more information you give me may not be applicable in court. Every bit of evidence we provide will be scrutinised by the defence team, and if your name is anywhere on that sheet, it could be disregarded."

Her eyes grew wide.

"So, I have to be careful here." His voice dropped a notch. "When I find the real killer, if apprehending them has anything even remotely to do with you, the case could be thrown out of court. It's imperative you are not involved in this investigation. Do you understand, Daisy?"

Okay, so maybe he had a point. She didn't want the killer to get off because she'd meddled in the case. But they might not catch the real killer unless she got involved. It was a tough call.

"I understand," she whispered.

He reached forward and wiped a strand of hair off her cheek. Daisy froze. It was the first real contact they'd had, and his hand felt warm and comforting against her skin. She stared at him, questions popping into her mind, but unable to find the words.

He didn't give her the chance. "I'll see you soon," he said, opening the door and disappearing out into the night.

Daisy stood inside the door listening as he got into his car and started the engine. It reversed slowly out of her driveway, the engine purring like an overgrown feline. She heard him put it in gear and take off down the road, the tyres scratching on the loose gravel.

Then she sighed and whispered to herself, "Sorry, Paul. My life is too important to sit this one out. I'm afraid you're stuck with me."

She'd just have to do it in such a way so as not to ruin the evidence. Her involvement must never be known.

Chapter Twelve

Daisy woke early, wrapped up warm, and set off for the salon. A thick layer of ice covered the windows of the cars in her lane, and the meadow opposite sparkled like a fairyland as the sun hit the frost. Her breath turned to steam as she walked. She'd texted Floria, Krish, Penny, and Asa last night and asked them to meet before work to discuss the next steps in their investigation. Her message had been short and perfunctory.

Paul wants to arrest me! We urgently need to find killer. Meet 7 am at Ooh La La?

They needed to figure this out before he followed through with his threat. Time was running out.

Waiting for her outside the double-glass doors were Krish and Penny, both flushed with cold and excitement. Asa arrived a few minutes later, eating an Egg McMuffin, and Floria waltzed in ten minutes after that, ready for battle. Beneath her winter coat, she wore frayed jeans, a pink shirt rolled up at the sleeves, and tennis shoes. "Let's get this show on the road," she declared, her blue eyes flashing. "We can't let Daisy go down for murder. Not on my watch!"

Daisy hugged her, then they sat down on the sofa. The others pulled up chairs and positioned them on the rug, their expressions earnest. Everybody was keen to get stuck in.

Daisy smiled around the group. "Thanks, guys. To fill you in, I had a visit from DCI McGuinness last night, and I'm officially the prime suspect in this case. I had the means, motive, and opportunity. It was my scissors that killed Melanie—which conveniently have my prints on them—I was alone in the salon when the murder took place, and now, thanks to my history with the victim, I apparently have motive."

"Your history with her?" Penny asked, her smooth brow crumpled in a frown.

"Yes, we were at school together."

"Melanie was a lying, backstabbing cow," cut in Floria, getting straight to the point. "She nicked Daisy's boyfriend when they were sixteen. On purpose."

Krish's eyes grew wide. "Oh my gosh. Is that for real? The little tart."

"I'm afraid so," Daisy confirmed, fidgeting on the sofa. Secondary school was not her finest moment, but it was essential her friends knew the truth. "And even though none of that matters now, it still gives me a motive, so unless we solve this case quickly and find out who really killed Melanie, it's going to be me sitting in that prison cell."

"I thought I was the chief suspect," whispered Penny.

"It was my scissors that killed her," Daisy pointed out. Her face fell. "Paul thinks the prosecution might have enough already to issue an arrest warrant. We don't have any time to lose."

Penny gasped, while Floria huffed. "Over my dead body."

"I'll visit you in the nick, Dais," said Asa, helpfully.

Krish elbowed her in the ribs.

"What? I'm just saying if she gets nicked, at least she'll have people to visit her. I visited my uncle Sol when he got knocked up on that dope charge. He really appreciated it."

"Thanks, Asa." Daisy grimaced. "Let's hope it doesn't come to that."

"So, where do we start?" Floria rubbed her hands together. "What do you want us to do?"

Daisy put her coffee cup down on the purple velvet footstool they used as a table. "Asa, didn't you tell me your cousin was an Uber driver?"

"Good memory." Asa stuffed the last of her breakfast muffin into her mouth. "But he works the Southwark area, not around here."

"Good enough. Can you ask him to try to get a hold of the Uber driver who picked up Liz Roberts the other night? We need to make sure she went straight home after she left the salon. We still can't be sure she didn't sneak around the back and lie in wait for Melanie."

Asa nodded. "Sure, I'll speak to him."

"I've written down the names of everyone who came in that day, including Yvette Bechard," said Penny, who liked lists. She took a folded A4 piece of paper out of her bag and spread it out next to Daisy's empty cup on the table.

"I think we need to revisit your three friends, Penny," said Daisy, pointing to Paloma, Apple, and Ferne's names. "Fancy a trip to the pub in Esher to speak to the barman? We need to check their alibis for Saturday night, even though I know you said they were there when you arrived."

"Sure, I'm up for that."

"Great." Daisy thought for a moment. "I wish I knew what Melanie was doing outside the salon on Saturday evening. Was she meeting someone? Was she waiting for me, perhaps?" She shrugged helplessly.

"It's a pity we can't see her phone records," said Krish. "That might give us a clue as to whom she was meeting. Maybe that dishy detective will show them to you?"

"Ha, fat chance," said Daisy with a laugh, then she sobered. "I can't be seen meddling in this case. He told me that because I'm the prime suspect, any evidence I provide will be questioned and probably thrown out of court."

"Then we have to keep you completely out of it," said Floria, her expression grim. "Maybe you should stay here and we'll report back."

"I have to live," Daisy insisted. "A drink at the pub is a normal thing to do, right?" At Floria's look, she added, "Don't worry, I won't be too obvious. I know what's at stake."

"I'll see what I can dig up," said Krish. "Mrs. Bryson is coming this afternoon. She's in the WI with Mel and Liz, and she might be able to shed some light on why Melanie came back here."

"That would be great," said Daisy, who never discounted local gossip. In her opinion, where there was smoke, there was usually fire. Especially in this little village.

"I'll visit Liz," said Floria. "I'll pretend to be scouting for business. I know that she and her husband entertain a lot. Perhaps they'd like me to arrange one of their dinner parties or a Christmas do, or something? You never know."

"Fabulous." Daisy beamed. "She'll be more than happy to talk to you. She was a great fan of your late mother. I remember how devastated she was when Dame Serena passed away."

Floria rolled her eyes.

"And . . ." continued Daisy, "she was upset when she came into the salon on Saturday evening. Apparently, it was to do with a guest speaker letting her down, but I'm not sure that was the truth."

"Not to mention how bizarrely happy she was to find out Mel was dead," added Krish, raising a finger. "That in itself is suspicious."

Daisy nodded. It sure was.

"Leave it with me," Floria reassured them. "I'll see what I can find out."

As they weren't busy, Daisy and Penny left work early and drove to Esher, where the hen party had taken place. The Bear was a historic pub that had been around for the better part of three hundred years. Originally a watering hole for travellers, it was now a stylish bar and restaurant with modern British cuisine and live music on weekends. Only the low wooden door and dark beams gave any indication of its past identity.

"Do you remember who served you?" asked Daisy as

they walked inside, ducking so as not to bump their heads. Penny, being five foot eleven, had to be extra careful.

Being a Wednesday evening, it was packed with a young, after-work crowd enjoying the fine ales on offer.

"Yes, Mickey and Stu were on duty," Penny said straightaway. At Daisy's surprised glance, she added, "Mickey's kind of cute and has a huge crush on Paloma, and Stu helped me in the loo with Apple when she was puking her guts out thanks to too many tequila shots."

"Sounds messy," remarked Daisy, as they headed to the bar.

"It was."

"Are either of them here?" Daisy eyed the two barmen, one who was making a complicated cocktail in a blender, and the other, who was pulling pints for a middle-aged gentleman.

"That's Mickey." Penny pointed to the cute guy pulling pints. He had long hair that fell over one eye, an aquiline nose, and a wide mouth.

"Great, let's go and have a chat," said Daisy.

Micky grinned the minute he saw Penny and held up a finger. "Give me a sec, gorgeous, and I'll be right with you." Daisy supposed that happened all the time when you were as beautiful as Penny.

True to his word, Mickey ignored the next customer and came over. "Hey, Penny, nice to see you back so soon." Penny leaned over the bar and kissed him on both cheeks. He looked at Daisy. "Who is your friend?"

"Daisy Thorne," said Daisy, holding out her hand. There would be no kissing here.

He shook it awkwardly, then looked back at Penny. "What can I get you?"

"Two glasses of dry white," she said with a smile, then under her voice to Daisy, "We'd better order a drink."

Daisy nodded. When he'd poured them, she asked, "Hey, Mickey, do you remember serving Penny and her friends on Saturday night?"

"Sure," he said with a broad smile. "It's hard to forget such lovely ladies."

"I got here late," Penny said, "but the others were already here. Do you know what time they arrived?"

He scrunched up his forehead. "Now you're asking me . . . Well, I came on duty at five, as per usual, and they weren't here then." He snapped his fingers. "Oh yeah, I was outside on my smoke break when the taxi dropped them off, so it must have been sevenish. They were already quite merry, if you catch my drift."

They'd probably been drinking since that morning in the hair salon. Daisy could only imagine the state of them by the end of the night. It was remarkable Paloma had managed to get to her own wedding the next day, let alone make it down the aisle.

"Oh, I know," said Penny.

He winked at her. "I hear you had your hands full with Apple in the loo. Pretty nasty."

Penny nodded.

"Were all three of them here the whole time?" asked Daisy.

"Mm . . ." He hesitated. "I think so. I served them a bottle of champagne, but I wasn't watching them the whole time, if you know what I mean. I had other customers too."

"Of course," said Daisy. "But you don't remember any of them disappearing around eight o'clock?"

He shook his head. "No, I don't think so, but like I said, it was very busy that night."

"Okay, thanks." Daisy felt a bit deflated. That wasn't the concise answer she'd been hoping for. They still couldn't be sure all three girls had remained at the pub during the course of the evening. Edgemead was only a ten-minute drive away at that time of night, less if you knew the back roads. Any one of them could have left the bar, driven to the salon, murdered Melanie, and made it back to the pub in under an hour. Even with the rain.

"I'm not sure Paloma, Apple, or Ferne were in any state to drive on Saturday night," said Penny, as they moved away from the bar and took a seat by the window. "Didn't Mickey say they arrived by cab?"

"Granted, it's not likely," admitted Daisy, sipping her wine. Outside, a continuous flow of cars eased by, and the windowpane turned from red to orange to green in the reflection of the traffic lights.

"So, how are things with Niall?" asked Daisy. She hadn't had a chance to talk to Penny about her relationship with the wealthy horse breeder lately. Daisy knew Niall fairly well, having met him several times at Floria's mother's house parties over the years. Dame Serena had been legendary for her summer soirees, which almost always ended in chaos and debauchery. Niall had been her third husband, and they'd remained friends after they'd split up. Daisy liked him, but having seen the women come and go over the years, she wasn't confident he was a good match for Penny. He was also much older than she was.

"Good," she said with an intimate smile. "We spent the day together on Sunday. I saw the little foal, she's too cute."

"I supposed Paul called him too?"

Penny rolled her eyes. "Yes, and Niall confirmed he'd cancelled on me, then told him where he could shove it." She laughed, and Daisy was glad to see she'd recovered some of her spark. DCI McGuinness had given her a terrible fright. At least Niall had stood up to him.

"I'm glad to hear it." Daisy suppressed a grin. "Paul wouldn't have liked that."

"Did you know he briefly dated Ferne?" Penny gazed into her wine.

"Who? Paul?" Daisy was momentarily thrown. She hadn't thought McGuinness the type to date a fashion model, but then she supposed he must have a private life. And why not a model?

"No, silly." Penny giggled. "Niall, not Paul."

"Oh." Daisy felt stupid but relieved. That made more sense. "No, I didn't know. Did he tell you that?"

"Yes, although Ferne has never mentioned it to me. He was dating her when I met him at Dame Serena's memorial service last year. I don't know what happened between them, but they broke up soon after that."

"Did he dump her for you?" asked Daisy. That would be a typical Niall move, always on to the next pretty girl.

Penny shook her head, her red hair wafting around her face. "Oh, gosh no. It was months later that he asked me out, and I still didn't accept straightaway. It took weeks of persuading before I agreed."

"Still, it must be hard for her to swallow," said Daisy. "I'm surprised she hasn't said anything to you."

"Well, we're not that close. She's more Paloma and Apple's friend than mine. I only know her through them. Anyway, she's dating a BBC sports presenter now, I believe. She was going on and on about him on Saturday night."

"Small world," murmured Daisy.

"How are things between you and Paul?" Penny enquired shyly. "He frightens me half to death, but I know you're fond of him. Did you date for a while?"

Daisy sighed. "Yes, but it never really got off the ground. I went to the south of France with Floria over the summer to sort out her father's estate, and we never met up again after that." It was as much her fault as it was his. She'd never called when she'd got back like she'd promised, and he'd been so busy thanks to his promotion and increased caseload that she hadn't wanted to disturb him.

"It's a shame. You guys make a good team."

"Except when he's threatening to arrest me," gritted Daisy.

"Well, yes. I suppose so. But it's obvious he likes you, Daisy. You're the only person who stands up to him. No one else could get away with what you do."

"He's not that scary." She smiled. "Although he'd be pretty annoyed with me if he knew I was still investigating this murder."

"Nobody knows you are," said Penny with a wink. "This is just a friendly drink."

"Absolutely," said Daisy. "It's just a pity we didn't get what we came for."

Chapter Thirteen

Daisy had just dropped Penny off at home when her phone rang. It was Krish. Putting it on speaker so she could drive, she answered, "Krish?"

"Oh my gosh, Daisy, you're never going to believe what I've discovered." His voice was unnaturally high, and he was breathing heavily down the line.

"What?" She flicked on her high beams as she wound her way along the narrow, meandering lanes that led to her cottage. There were no streetlamps in this part of the countryside, so the roads were pitch-dark. Added to that, the cows in the nearby meadow had a dangerous habit of wandering into the streets whenever the farmer left the gate open.

"I've just come from the rugby club, where I discovered that Melanie Haverstock was having an affair with Liz Roberts's husband, the dog-food billionaire!"

It took a moment for his words to sink in. Then she pulled off the road onto a grassy verge and put her hazard lights on. "Holy crap! Krish, this is huge. Are you sure?"

"Totally. I heard it from Bob Newman, the chairman himself."

Daisy's heart was pounding. If it was true, it gave Liz an undeniable motive.

"You still there?" he asked, after a beat.

"Yes, sorry. I'm just in shock. Melanie kept that awfully quiet, didn't she?"

"Well, it's out now."

"Why am I not surprised?" Daisy tapped her fingers on the steering wheel. "Melanie never changed."

"Nope, we should have guessed it was something like this that got her killed. After your story—"

"Yes, quite," Daisy interrupted, not keen to revisit that particular episode. "What are you doing at the rugby club? It's not one of your usual haunts."

Krish chuckled. "No, but there's a hot, young centre-forward with very reassuring thighs that I'm chatting up, and he's good friends with the chairman, who is very good friends with Mr. Roberts. After a few pints, the old guy told us everything."

A thought struck her, and she gasped. "Krish, do you think Mel was meeting him on Saturday night? Perhaps that's where she was going when she was killed."

"Could be," Krish agreed.

"Do you know how long the affair has been going on? And more importantly, did poor Douglas know? Because if he did, then he must surely be a suspect too." Her mind was racing now.

"Hey, slow down, Miss Sherlock. As far as I can gather, the affair started a few months ago. Bob said Roy began disappearing after matches on Saturdays instead of joining them for drinks at the clubhouse. He was most put out by it 'cause he lost his drinking buddy."

"Maybe Melanie was with him on Saturday afternoon," Daisy mused, glancing in her rearview mirror. There was nothing coming, so she pulled back out into the lane. "That could be why she told her husband she was going to that book launch at the library."

"Book launch?" asked Krish.

"There wasn't one." Her cottage appeared on the left, so she signalled and turned into her driveway but didn't cut the engine. "We need to find out whether Liz took that Uber or not," said Daisy, with a sudden surge of energy. It was hard to picture the posh, coiffed Liz Roberts, head of the prestigious Women's Institute, stabbing Melanie in the back, but stranger things had happened. Perhaps she'd lost her renowned control and been eaten up by rage caused by her husband's affair.

"Asa said she was going to speak to her cousin tonight," said Krish, who'd locked up the salon because Daisy and Penny had left early to go to Esher.

"Okay, good." There wasn't much they could do tonight. She said goodbye to Krish and climbed out of her car. She ought to have left the outside light on. It was pitch-dark, and even the crescent moon was enveloped by hulking storm clouds. Daisy was inching her way to the front door when she heard a rustle in the bushes behind her. She spun around but couldn't see anything in the darkness.

"Hello?" she called.

No answer.

Had she imagined it? Erring on the side of caution, she decided not to investigate the sound. That's what they always did in the movies, and it never turned out well. Daisy always wanted to yell at the TV in frustration. She wouldn't fall into that trap, just in case there was someone out there.

Hurrying now, she inserted her house key in the lock and went inside. The cottage was in darkness. She flicked the switch and closed the door behind her, making sure to draw the bolt across. It had been a long day, she was overwrought, and it was probably just Moira's cat from next door. She took off her coat and hung it on the hook, and that was when she saw it. A note had been pushed through the slot in her front door.

Slowly, she bent down to pick it up. It was written on unlined white paper, about half the size of an A4 page. On it, someone had scrawled: *MURDERER.*

Gasping, she dropped the note on the kitchen counter and fumbled for her phone.

DCI McGuinness answered on the second ring. "Daisy? What's up?"

Gone were the days when she could give him a social call. Now if she rang him, it was because something was up.

"Paul, someone left me a note. It says 'murderer' on it."

A pause. "I'll come over. Don't touch it."

"I've picked it up, but that's all."

"Okay, I'll be there as soon as I can."

He must have flown along the motorway, blue lights flashing, because he made it to her cottage in under half an hour. On a good day, Guildford was forty-five minutes away.

"Where is it?" he asked as soon as she opened the door.

"On the countertop." She pointed to where she'd thrown it. He pulled on forensic gloves and picked it up, inspecting it on both sides. The offending word was handwritten in capital letters in thick, black ink.

"There seems to be some sort of watermark on it," Daisy pointed out. "It looks like a fleur-de-lis, but I can't quite make it out."

"I'll have it analysed," he muttered, placing the note in a clear plastic evidence bag. "But somebody thinks you're responsible."

"Do you think it's the murderer, trying to make me look guilty?" If she got threatening notes, other people might think she had something to hide.

"Possibly." He scratched his chin. It was covered in stubble after a very long day. It kind of suited him, made him look a bit rough around the edges, not so official. "Or it might be a disgruntled member of the community. We can't know for sure, but I'll have it dusted for prints."

"I thought I heard someone outside when I got back tonight," Daisy told him. "I probably disturbed them when I turned into the driveway."

Paul frowned. "Did you see anyone?"

She shook her head. "Just a rustle in the bushes. It could have been Mr. Tiddles, the neighbour's cat."

"I'm not sure you should be alone right now, Daisy. Is there anyone who can stay with you?"

"No, not really. I could stay at Brompton Court with Floria and Josh," she said, but the thought of getting into the car and driving back towards Esher again wasn't appealing. "I'm sure it'll be fine. If someone was going to harm me, they wouldn't have bothered to leave a note."

He gave her a wry look. "The two aren't necessarily connected."

Daisy's eyes widened. "You mean the rustle in the bushes might not have been the person who left the note?" She hadn't thought about it like that.

"Regardless of who left the note, the real killer is still out there," said McGuinness. "And he or she may have set their sights on you."

"I don't think so," she said, frowning. "Why would they use my scissors, then? If they killed me, they'd have no scapegoat."

McGuinness regarded her silently.

Then she remembered the phone call with Krish. "Oh my goodness. I forgot to tell you. Melanie was having an affair with Liz Roberts's husband."

The detective stared at her for a long moment, then said, "I thought I told you to stay out of this investigation."

She gritted her teeth. "I wasn't investigating, I swear. This didn't come from me."

"Hmm . . ." He sat down on the armchair he'd used the night before, his long legs stretched out in front of him. He still had his coat on, and although he looked weary, his eyes flickered with interest. "You'd better tell me how you came upon this information."

Daisy perched on the sofa, pulling a scatter cushion

onto her lap. After the fright of the note, she needed something reassuring to hold on to, and DCI McGuinness didn't look like he was offering.

"Bob Newman, chairman of the Edgemead Rugby Club, told Krish about the affair earlier this evening, and he called me as soon as he could. I've only just spoken to him. I was about to call you when I saw the note."

He nodded, and she exhaled. At least he believed her. "And he's absolutely certain?"

"Yes, but even if he wasn't, it's still worth checking out. If Melanie was sleeping with Liz's husband—and I wouldn't put it past her, she had a nasty habit of poaching other women's men—that would give Liz the perfect motive for murder."

"It also puts Mr. Haverstock back in the picture." McGuinness sighed.

"Yes, I suppose so, but I still don't think Douglas had anything to do with it." But she was glad that she and Penny had shifted further down on the official suspects list. "I know real grief when I see it."

"I've known killers who murdered partners they were in love with," he said sombrely. "Their grief is real, but so is their anger."

Daisy didn't reply. She couldn't argue with that. Had Douglas murdered Melanie out of rage because she'd been having an affair? The tepid accountant who didn't like to go out? Had he finally cracked and killed his vivacious wife? No, she just couldn't see it, and how would he have gotten access to her cutting scissors?

"It's more likely Liz found out about their relationship and decided to do something about it. She's not the type of woman to take that sort of thing on the chin. I wouldn't be surprised if she stole my scissors that evening, then snuck around the back and killed Melanie. And come to think of it, she was inordinately happy to discover Melanie was dead."

"What do you mean?" McGuinness perked up at that.

"She came into the salon on Monday demanding to know if Melanie really was dead. When I said yes, she smiled, and bounced out of there like I'd made her day. It was very strange."

"That definitely warrants further investigation," McGuinness said. "I'll bring her in for questioning tomorrow."

Daisy yawned. She wanted to go to bed, but it was so reassuring having Paul there. After the surprise note and their consequent discussion, she was a little on edge. As if reading her mind, McGuinness got up and checked the windows. "Make sure everything is securely fastened," he said, "and I'm glad you got this dead bolt on the door."

"Yes, I had that installed last year," she admitted. "Before we knew who killed Serena."

"Do you want me to check upstairs before I go?" he asked.

"Yes, please." It would put her mind at rest, not that she was expecting anyone to be hiding under the bed.

After a thorough check, he returned downstairs. "All good. Well, I'll leave you to it. It's getting late, and I'd best be off." He still had to drive back to Guildford tonight. She wondered what his house looked like. They'd always met in Edgemead, and she was curious to see how he lived. Not that she'd ever find out now. DCI "By the Book" McGuinness wasn't the type to date a suspect in a murder inquiry. There was more chance of him having a relationship with a fashion model.

"Thank you, Paul."

"Good night, Daisy." He hesitated briefly at the door, as if he wanted to say something else, but then decided against it. "Sleep well."

She shut the door after him and drew the bolt across. At least her cottage was intruder-free, but somehow, she didn't think sleep was going to come very easily tonight.

Chapter Fourteen

Daisy was up to her elbows in tint when Asa rushed in, late as usual, flushed with excitement. She tripped over the rug in the entrance to the salon and nearly went flying in her haste to get to Daisy.

"Asa, stop. Take a breath." Daisy held up a gloved hand as her assistant skidded to a halt, panting.

"I've got . . . I've got . . ." She was breathing so hard she couldn't get the words out.

"Give me five minutes, and I'll meet you in the kitchen," said Daisy, who didn't want to talk in front of the customers. It was bad enough that rumours about her and Penny were flying around the village; she didn't need to add fuel to the fire.

Asa paused, exhaled, then nodded and sashayed off to set up the nail bar. Five minutes later, Daisy glanced over, but the nail technician had a queue waiting. The Halloween rush didn't let up until sometime later, and it was nearly midday before Daisy had time to sit with Asa and hear her news.

"Please tell me your cousin was able to find something out for us?"

"He asked around," Asa said, reaching for the biscuit tin Daisy kept in the kitchen cupboard for emergencies. Some days they were so busy they didn't get time to eat. Asa's nails were a glossy black with white spiderwebs strewn across them. It looked very professional. "And finally tracked down the cabbie who drove Mrs. Roberts home on Saturday night."

"Yes?" Daisy could hardly contain her curiosity. Had Liz gone straight home or not?

"She did get the Uber at eight thirty-five," said Asa. "The driver, Eddie Grant, said she ran out of the store like the clappers on account of the rain and jumped into the cab."

"Crap. It couldn't have been her, then." Daisy's shoulders sagged. Her number-one suspect's alibi checked out.

"No, but there's something else."

"Oh?" Daisy glanced up.

"When Eddie dropped her at home, Mr. Roberts was getting out of his car. It looked like he'd just gotten back himself. According to Eddie, there was an awful row. The two of them were screaming at each other like you wouldn't believe. She went at him hammer and tongs, even smacked him in the face."

"Really? Liz actually hit him?" Daisy could not picture the snobby, sophisticated Liz behaving like a harridan. She was always so controlled.

Asa nodded, chewing on her biscuit, her eyes gleaming. "Yeah, Eddie said it was crazy. He left after that, but I reckon things must have been pretty intense in their house over the weekend."

"She knows about the affair," murmured Daisy, reaching for a biscuit. "Why else would they be fighting?"

Krish chose that moment to come into the kitchen. "Lavinia Marcus has just arrived for her cut and blow. Bianca is giving her a shampoo and conditioning treatment. What did you find out, Asa?"

She relayed the news to him, while Daisy crunched her biscuit, deep in thought.

"Of course, she knows," agreed Krish. "The wife always knows."

"I think we can assume Melanie was with Mr. Roberts on Saturday afternoon, before she was killed. Then she came back to the salon for some unknown reason, while her lover went home to be confronted by his wife."

"Who knew exactly what he'd been up to," finished Krish, waving a finger in the air.

"Except Liz didn't kill her," pointed out Asa. "She didn't have time."

"No," mused Daisy. "I was here when she left the salon a little after eight-thirty, and now, thanks to Eddie, we know she got straight into that Uber. She didn't want to mess her hair up."

"Fair enough," reasoned Krish.

"What we need to find out," mused Daisy, "is what Mel was doing back here on Saturday night."

"It's a mystery," said Krish, hearing the bell above the door tinkle and going out to see to their next customer. Daisy put the kettle on. Lavinia Marcus appreciated jasmine green tea when she was having her cut and blow-dry.

"I'd better get back to work." Asa stuffed one more biscuit into her mouth and disappeared out the door.

Daisy made Lavinia's tea, then took it to her on a small silver tray.

"Hello, Daisy. It's good to see you," gushed a pink-cheeked Lavinia. "I heard about what happened—absolutely appalling, and to think you were questioned too. What were those policemen thinking?"

Daisy didn't know what to say. She opened her mouth to reply, but Lavinia pressed on. "If it's any consolation, I don't believe a word of it. As I told Dr. Kendal, the vet, that Daisy Thorne is such a sweetie and not at all the murdering type. She always makes me a nice cup of tea when I arrive for my appointment. What cold-blooded killer would do that?"

"Why, thank you, Lavinia," Daisy said, not sure about the logic of her argument, but it was nice to know someone was on her side. A couple more customers had cancelled their appointments, so their diary had lightened even more. Daisy only hoped that once this nasty business was over and the real killer was caught, things would get back to normal. The whole village was a hotspot for gossip. Small-town syndrome, she supposed. But it didn't sit well.

"The usual?" she asked Lavinia, who nodded brightly.

"Please. And tell me, has that lovely detective McGregor been in lately? He's so . . . competent, isn't he?" She shivered with anticipation. "Quite the dish."

"It's McGuinness, actually, and no, not today, I'm afraid." It seemed half the village was in love with Paul McGuinness, the other half terrified of him. He was certainly a man who evoked strong emotions in people. As for competent, well, that remained to be seen.

* * *

At lunchtime, Daisy popped out to grab a sandwich and coffee. The high street was buzzing with people and traffic. It seemed to get busier towards the end of the week, and this weekend was Halloween. The Party Palace a bit farther up on the right was doing a roaring trade as mothers splurged on kiddie's costumes and adults purchased suitably spooky outfits and wigs for their grown-up parties. She was about to cross the busy road, when she spotted Krish with a beefy giant of a man coming out of the shop. The stylist was carrying a Frankenstein mask, while the giant held a scythe. Daisy waved, but they didn't see her; they were too busy laughing over some private joke. It was great Krish had a new love interest. He'd been devastated when his last boyfriend had turned out to be married with a wife and two young children. "I won't be some confused middle-aged man's boy toy," he'd huffed, when he'd told them what had happened. "He can have his epiphany with someone else." The dark mood had lasted several weeks, until he'd met the rugby player.

Starbucks was heaving, so she got her pumpkin-spiced latte and a sandwich and sat in the corner by the window mulling over what Asa had told her. Liz knew about her husband's affair with Melanie, and knowing Liz, the feisty head of the Women's Institute wouldn't have put up with that. In fact, she was willing to bet good money that Liz had demanded her husband end the affair or else . . . Or else what? Would she have resorted to murder? Daisy chewed her sandwich while she pondered this. Liz certainly had it in her to commit murder. She was cool, calm, and collected, always the epitome of political correctness, never putting a foot wrong, but Daisy knew how highly she valued her reputation. Image was everything to her, and she wouldn't allow anything or anyone to tarnish it. Daisy let out an exasperated sigh. Except she couldn't have done it because she'd gone straight home that night to confront her husband.

Daisy had finished her coffee and lunch when, through the window, she saw a stocky man with ginger hair and a face not unlike a bulldog leaving Yvette's boutique. He walked with purpose, his features scrunched up in the middle of his face, and his shoulders pushed forward in a threatening manner. Alarm bells went off in her head.

Rushing into Yvette's store, she found the Frenchwoman in a heap on the floor behind the counter. She was sobbing, holding a tissue to her nose.

"Did he hurt you?" Daisy asked, bending down beside her. "Because if he did . . ."

She shook her head but didn't stop blubbering.

Daisy was momentarily confounded. Yvette was usually so composed; this breakdown was completely out of character for her. The man must have really frightened her.

"Who was he, Yvette?" she asked, putting an arm around the distraught woman.

She glanced up, her eyes bloodshot. "He . . . He wants to buy the boutique. I keep telling him it's not for sale, but he won't give up."

"Have you told the police about this?" she said. It was a clear case of harassment.

"*Non.*" Then she started crying again.

"Why is he pestering you, Yvette?" asked Daisy.

"He knows the boutique is going under." She sniffed and wiped her eyes. The tissues were piling up on the floor beside her. "I can't pay next month's rent."

"Oh, I'm so sorry," murmured Daisy. She'd suspected as much, but the situation was obviously worse than she thought. "Is there nothing you can do?"

"I've tried everything," said Yvette, struggling to her feet. Daisy gave her a hand up. "But unless I get a backer, I'm going to have to sell."

Daisy was silent for a moment. Yvette straightened her dress, then took yet another tissue and blew her nose.

"You aren't prepared to consider his offer?" she asked, eventually.

"That man is a pig," hissed Yvette. "I would rather sell my body than give the boutique to him. Do you know what he wants to do with my store? He wants to turn it into a betting shop." She spat the words out like it was a fate worse than death.

Oh dear. The last thing this town needed was another betting shop. There were already two in the parade behind the station, and frankly, it lowered the tone of the whole village. "Well, let's hope it doesn't come to that," breathed Daisy.

Yvette sniffed. "And after everything I've done here. Ten years of hard work. I can't . . . I can't . . . let it go." She dissolved into tears again.

Daisy patted her back. This wouldn't do at all.

"What is that man's name, Yvette?" If she told McGuinness, maybe he could get the bulldog to back off.

She shrugged. "He calls himself Olaf, but he's just a thug. Betting Direct is the company who wants to buy me out."

Daisy blew a hair off her face. Betting Direct was one of the largest bookies in the country. Yvette wouldn't have much luck fighting them off.

"I need a miracle," she moaned.

"Let's get a cup of tea," said Daisy, who was still full from the pumpkin latte. "Shall we pop over to Paul's? My treat."

They were more likely to get a table at Paul's because it was one of the most expensive cafés on the high street. It served a selection of French pastries and coffee from Brazil, and Daisy had seen Yvette come out of it on more than one occasion. It would also be quiet enough to talk. The Frenchwoman perked up. "Okay," she said, "but give me a moment to sort myself out. I can't go looking like this."

Daisy waited while she popped to the bathroom at the back of the store. Glancing around, she spotted a pile of unopened post on the countertop. A folded-up note in the middle caught her eye.

She reached for it, heart hammering, and slowly unfolded it.

Murderer was handwritten across the top.

Daisy gasped. It was identical to the note she'd received, written on the same thick card and with the same felt-tip pen. It even sported the same faded watermark in the top right corner. She stared at it for a long moment. Had Yvette seen it yet? It had been lying amidst several unopened envelopes on the counter next to the cash register as if Yvette had picked up the post that morning and dumped it on the table to open at a later date. With a bit of luck, she hadn't seen it yet. The door to the bathroom opened, and Daisy popped the note into her pocket. Yvette was upset enough already, she didn't need to be told she was a murderer too. A flash of anger sizzled up Daisy's spine. How dare the perpetrator terrorise the residents of Edgemead in this manner? People like Yvette had enough to deal with without worrying about being labelled a murderer. What could he hope to prove by it? Well, this little stunt had failed, because Daisy was not going to let Yvette see it. Whoever had sent the poisonous note wasn't going to get the reaction they'd hoped for.

When Yvette returned, she'd reapplied her makeup and turned back into the elegant boutique owner Daisy knew. There was even a faint blush to her cheeks, which was mostly makeup, but so expertly done that it gave her a natural and healthy glow.

"Ready?" asked Daisy, her voice overly bright.

Yvette nodded. She didn't once glance towards the counter or the other pile of post, so Daisy was fairly certain she was unaware of the note.

Over steaming cups of English breakfast tea, Daisy asked Yvette to tell her when her business had started to run into trouble. Although the murderous note was burning a hole in her coat pocket, she thought it wiser to get Yvette over this crisis before she dumped another one in her lap. Of course, she was going to tell her about the note. Eventually. But right now, giving it to Yvette would achieve nothing—and it would play into the sender's hands.

"About a year ago," Yvette replied, her shoulders sagging, "when the big Sainsbury's started supplying clothes along with groceries. And then Dame Serena died and her daughter donated her entire wardrobe to Oxfam. Nobody came near my store for months, even though I have all the latest French fashions."

Daisy cringed. Floria was her best friend, but they'd been oblivious to the effect the donation would have on Yvette's boutique.

"And then it got worse. Everybody is shopping online or going into central London. There is no need for my petite boutique anymore."

"You are very niche," Daisy agreed. "But perfect for when one needs something and doesn't have time to go into London or wait for an online delivery. I'm not sure what we'd do without you."

"I wish everyone thought that way." Yvette snivelled, but now that her makeup had been carefully reapplied, Daisy thought it unlikely she'd erupt into tears again. Her pride wouldn't allow it.

"Can I get you anything else, ladies?" asked the manager, a well-dressed man with floppy hair and a charming smile.

"No thanks, Pierre," said Yvette, absently patting his hand. His face lit up at the contact.

"He seems nice." Daisy smiled as he walked away, still grinning.

Yvette perked up. "Oh yes. Pierre is a sweetie. I've known him for years. He's been here ever since Paul's opened in Edgemead."

"That was about five years ago, wasn't it?" asked Daisy, her forehead furrowing. She'd opened her salon around the same time. The high street had seen a lot of changes since then. They'd gotten some fancy restaurants, an upmarket Chinese takeaway, a Starbucks, even a McDonald's, although that was down the other end by the station. There was an Irish pub that was popular with the horse-racing crowd, as well as several English pubs that showed the rugby and football fixtures every weekend, many of whom did a decent Sunday roast. Yes, Edgemead had come a long way since she'd set up shop.

"Something like that," Yvette acknowledged. "It will be a shame to leave Edgemead. This is my home now."

"Do you have to leave?"

She nodded sadly. "Douglas tells me I have one more month at the most, then I will have to sell. I'll take what money I get for it and move into the city." She shrugged. "I have to work."

Daisy wondered why Yvette had never married. She was in her late thirties, maybe even early forties, judging by the number of grey hairs hidden under that glossy brown sheen, but it was hard to know for sure. She was so well-groomed that she appeared ageless.

Wait a minute! "Did you say Douglas?"

"Yes, he is my accountant."

"Douglas Haverstock?"

"Yes, is there a problem with that? He is a very nice man, unlike his wife." She said something rather rude in French.

Daisy's eyebrows shot up. "You didn't like Melanie, either?"

Yvette made a distinctly unladylike sound. "She used to come into my boutique and flaunt her money around. I think she enjoyed humiliating me."

"She knew you were having financial difficulties?"

Yvette shrugged. "Of course. Her husband is my accountant." Then she looked directly at Daisy. "I'm not sorry she's dead. She was a horrible woman."

Daisy didn't disagree. It seemed Melanie had been up to her old tricks, bullying those less fortunate and stealing other people's husbands. Who else had she hacked off?

"Have you told DCI McGuinness about this?" she asked.

Yvette narrowed her eyes. "*Non*. Why would I do that?"

Daisy shrugged. "It's not important." She didn't want to upset Yvette anymore. Pierre came back to clear their table, and Daisy smiled her thanks. "I've got to get back to the salon, Yvette, but I hope you're feeling a bit better now?"

"I am, *merci*, Daisy." She gave Daisy's hand a squeeze, then crossed the road and went back to her boutique.

Daisy didn't want to betray her confidence, but McGuinness ought to know about Melanie's badgering. If for no other reason than it gave Yvette a motive.

Chapter Fifteen

Daisy entered Ooh La La to find Liz Roberts sitting on the sofa waiting for her. The formidable head of the Women's Institute was reading a copy of Vogue magazine, her long, manicured fingers half-heartedly flicking through the pages. She got to her feet as soon as Daisy walked in.

"Liz," Daisy said, taking off her coat and rubbing her hands together to warm them up. Her gloves were still in evidence with the police, and she was beginning to doubt she'd ever get them back. "This is a surprise."

"Is there somewhere we can talk?" asked Liz in a hushed tone, dispensing with the small talk. She looked paler than usual beneath her makeup, and she'd chewed off most of the lipstick on her lower lip.

"Um, sure, give me a minute." Daisy asked Penny to see to her next customer, who'd been shampooed and was waiting for her at a workstation, then went back to Liz. "We can talk in the kitchen."

The tiny kitchen had become the hub of the investigation. Penny's list of suspects was stuck inside the cupboard that housed the teacups, so she must be careful not to open it in front of Liz. It wouldn't do for the president of the WI to see her name near the top. Even if it had been crossed out of late.

"What is it?" asked Daisy, once they'd closed the door. Under normal circumstances she'd offer Liz a cup of tea, but after that spiced pumpkin latte and the English breakfast tea at Paul's, Daisy didn't think she could stomach any more.

Liz pulled a folded-up note from her handbag and handed it to Daisy. "I found this in my post box this afternoon."

Daisy's pulse ticked up a notch. Liz had received a threatening note too. Slowly, she opened it, careful to keep her expression neutral. Sure enough, the word *MURDERER* was written across the top in the now-familiar thick black ink. Once again, the watermark was present.

"What does it mean?" Liz whispered, her eyes boring into Daisy's.

Daisy's mind went into overdrive. Was the person responsible randomly sending a note to everyone who might have had an opportunity to murder Melanie? And if so, what was their aim? To deflect suspicion off themselves or confuse the investigation by misleading the police? Or was there another reason she hadn't thought of yet?

"I don't know." Daisy turned the note over and inspected the back before returning it to Liz. It was blank, just like hers and Yvette's. "How do you know it's for you and not your husband?"

"Because Roy's not home during the day. He works in the city, so he leaves early and gets back after seven. They must have known I'd find it."

She had a point. None of the notes were addressed to anyone in particular, but they had been left in such a way that the intended person would find them. Hers through her front door, Yvette's at the boutique, and Liz's at her house.

"We should call the police," Daisy said. Now that Yvette and Liz had received notes, she ought to tell McGuinness. As far as she knew, he hadn't found any fingerprints on hers, but that wasn't to say the sender hadn't left prints on these.

"Oh no." Liz gasped. "I don't want to do that. That's why I came to you, Daisy. You're discreet." She gripped Daisy's hand. "All that business with Dame Serena last year, you were brilliant. And you helped solve the crime. I want you to find out who sent me this."

"I'm not an investigator," Daisy pointed out, gently retrieving her hand. "And DCI McGuinness will be very upset if I go poking my nose into his investigation." Not that he wasn't already. Imagine what he'd say if he discovered she was withholding evidence.

"Please, Daisy," begged Liz. "There is no one else I can turn to." Her voice dropped a few notches. "I know why they sent me this."

"You do?"

"Yes, it's because . . ." She broke off, her hand fluttering to the strand of pearls around her neck. A flush crept into her pale cheeks. "It's because Roy was having an affair with Melanie Haverstock."

Daisy didn't reply.

"Please don't tell," Liz went on, oblivious to Daisy's lack of reaction. "I couldn't bear for anyone to find out. It's bad enough the police know."

"They do?" McGuinness hadn't wasted much time in contacting Liz after their chat last night.

"Yes, and I don't want that brute of a detective questioning me again. I drove all the way to Guildford to give a statement this morning—voluntarily, I might add—and he stuck me in a sordid interview room like a common criminal." She pulled a face like she'd caught a whiff of a bad smell.

Daisy knew what that felt like.

"They think I did it, you see. They think I killed that awful woman." She reached into her purse for a tissue, and Daisy noticed her hand was shaking. The "murder" note, or maybe it was the interrogation by McGuinness this morning, had left the normally stoic Liz more shaken than Daisy had ever seen her.

"But you went straight home on Saturday night when you left here, didn't you?" Daisy knew the answer, but she wanted to hear Liz say it. She was a great believer in getting information directly from the source.

"Yes, it was pouring with rain. The Uber was outside when I left. I didn't even know Melanie was going to be here."

No one did. That was the strange thing.

"Did Roy know that you knew about the affair?" Daisy asked, wanting to confirm what Eddie the Uber driver had said about the row she'd had with her husband when she got home.

"He does now," she said bitterly.

Daisy could only imagine the strain their relationship was under.

"It's intolerable, the thought of him with that . . . that tart. She parades around like she's a common prostitute in those skintight dresses and high heels." She shuddered. "It's unbearable."

"Not anymore," Daisy whispered.

Liz glanced up. "Well, yes. Quite." She couldn't quite prevent the gleam that appeared in her eye, or maybe that was unshed tears. "It doesn't change the fact that it happened, however."

Daisy had to admit she was right about that.

"You could always leave him," she said.

"Heavens, no," blurted Liz, horrified at the thought. "Imagine what people would say! And I don't want to live alone. Roy and I have been married for eighteen years. We have three kids together, it would destroy them. No, it's out of the question. I won't get divorced."

Daisy wondered if Roy felt the same way. Maybe now that Melanie was dead, he'd find solace in the arms of his wife again. For Liz's sake, she hoped so.

She sighed. "Okay. Leave this with me, and I'll see what I can find out."

Liz prided herself on her stellar reputation. If the citizens of Edgemead thought Liz Roberts was a jealous wife who'd murdered her husband's lover, she'd never be able to look anyone in the eye again. Liz considered herself to be an upstanding member of the community. She worked tirelessly for the Women's Institute and prided herself on being someone people looked up to. The Robertses lived in a sprawling seven-bedroom house on the outskirts of town and hosted the annual Best Garden award ceremony every summer. Roy Roberts was on a first-name basis with the mayor. A scandal like this would destroy her.

"Oh, thank you, Daisy." Liz clutched her hand. "I knew I could count on you."

Daisy walked Liz to the front door. As she was saying goodbye, Liz leaned forward and whispered, "Have you heard? Yvette's boutique is shutting down. I believe Betting Direct has made her an offer." She crinkled her nose. "Just what we need, another bookie."

"How do you know that?" enquired Daisy. Was nothing sacred in this town?

"Roy told me. Anyway, I saw that awful representative of theirs, Olaf, with Melanie the other day. He's a thug if I ever saw one, and thick as thieves, they were. I'm sure she told Olaf what dire straits the boutique was in. Mark my words, that woman was a nasty piece of work."

Daisy had to admit it did sound like something Melanie would do. And she would have known about the state of the boutique, thanks to her husband, who was doing the books. So, it was Melanie who'd put the wolves on Yvette. Now, that was interesting. Unfortunately for Yvette, she was looking more and more like a likely suspect.

"Penny, can I have a word?" said Daisy, once Liz had gone.

Penny, who had finished Lavinia's hair and was about to start on a new customer, stopped what she was doing and followed Daisy into the kitchenette. "How well do you know Yvette?" Daisy asked.

"Fairly well," said Penny with a fond smile. "I've been into her boutique quite a few times lately, and we often discuss the latest fashions and trends. She likes to keep up-to-date."

Daisy told her what Liz Roberts had said about Melanie and Olaf. Penny was shocked. "Do you think Yvette had something to do with Melanie's death?"

"I don't know, but we need to find out if she has an alibi for Saturday night." She didn't tell Penny about the note Yvette had received, or the one Liz had given her, both of which were hidden in her coat pocket. If she told them about the notes, she'd have to admit she had received one, too, which wasn't a problem amongst her friends, but if it got out . . . The salon was in enough difficulty already, now that customers were getting cold feet.

"Isn't that the detective's job?" asked Penny.

"Yes, but then I'd have to tell him what I just told you, and if Yvette's innocent, it will be awful for her. You know how intimidating DCI McGuinness can be." If the stalwart Liz could be reduced to a shaking shell of her former self, then what chance did the rest of them have?

"Oh yes," said Penny, nodding. "Okay, I'll pop around there this afternoon and see what I can find out."

"Perhaps if you mention the murder and tell her how you were questioned, she might volunteer the information." It was a long shot, but it could work.

"Okay," said Penny. "I'll go after work. I finish at five today, and I know Yvette's open until six."

"Perfect." Daisy got back to business. They had a flurry of customers, so she didn't have time to think about the case anymore until almost four thirty. Krish was finishing up their last customer when a shiny black BMW pulled up outside the salon. It was the flashing lights that got her attention. They penetrated the glass windows that faced the road and bounced off the walls like a colourful strobe.

DCI McGuinness.

It must be urgent because he'd ramped the pavement in a no parking zone, making no attempt to disguise his presence or preserve her privacy. Great, now the entire high street knew the police were here. He marched inside, sending the little bell into a frenzy of tingling, Buckley close on his heels. With his pinched expression and black coat flowing out behind him, he appeared very formidable. Daisy froze. This wasn't good.

"Detective, what can I do for you?"

Asa edged behind the basins while Penny gazed at him in alarm, and Krish, along with his bemused customer, stared with open curiosity.

McGuinness took a deep breath. "Daisy Thorne, I'm arresting you on suspicion of murdering Melanie Haverstock. You do not have to say anything, but it may harm your defence if you do not mention when questioned something that you later rely on in court. Anything you do say may be given in evidence."

Asa gave a loud screech and ran into the kitchen, while Krish stood rooted to the spot, mouthing like a guppy. His customer gasped and put her hand over her mouth. Penny came forward and took Daisy's arm.

"No," she whispered to the detective. "You've made a terrible mistake."

"What is going on, Paul?" Daisy asked quietly.

"We got the lab results back," he said. "You had Melanie's DNA on your gloves and the sleeves of your coat. I'm afraid I have no choice but to arrest you."

Chapter Sixteen

"Handcuffs? Really?" Daisy searched McGuinness's face for a sign that he was joking, that this was a horrendous mistake, but he remained impassive. Damn, he hid his emotions well.

"It's protocol," was all he said as he clipped the steel cuffs around her wrists. Buckley patted her down for weapons and removed the two folded notes from her coat pocket. Wordlessly, he handed them to McGuinness.

The detective's eyes narrowed as he opened them. Daisy held her breath.

"Two more?" he asked her.

"They're not mine."

He frowned. "Whose are they?"

She opened her mouth to explain when he held up a hand. "You know what, we can do this at the station."

She closed her mouth again. McGuinness turned away, his back rigid, and marched to the car. "Bring her," he told Buckley.

Penny was white-faced. "Daisy, what shall I do?"

Daisy thought fast. "Call Donna and tell her what's happened. Get Greg to meet me at the Guildford Police Department." Greg would know what to do. Even though he was the Levanté family solicitor and a trust attorney, he'd be able to advise her and help her get legal representation if need be. Besides, it wouldn't hurt to have some backup when she faced off with McGuinness. Part of her still hoped this was all some horrid misunderstanding and would be sorted out once she'd got to the station.

As she sat in the back of DCI McGuinness's stealthy, black BMW next to a female police officer, she racked her brains to figure out how Melanie's DNA had gotten on her gloves and jacket. She definitely hadn't touched the body at the crime scene, other than to trip over it in the pouring rain, so it must have happened earlier in the day. She understood Locard's exchange principle from the criminology diploma she was working toward, that every contact by a criminal leaves behind a trace, except in this case she wasn't a criminal and she hadn't touched the victim.

McGuinness drove all the way to Guildford in stony silence, not once glancing in the rearview mirror at her, even though she was sitting right behind him. He was livid, she could tell. His neck muscles were rigid, and his hands gripped the steering wheel so hard his knuckles had turned white. Not only did it appear she'd lied about handling the body, but she'd also withheld important evidence. To be fair, she'd only been given the two murder notes that morning, and they'd been busy with back-to-back customers all afternoon. There simply hadn't been time to call him and arrange a meeting. Not that any of that mattered now.

They arrived in Guildford, and McGuinness pulled up directly in front of the police department. To her surprise, it was a modern brick, chrome, and glass building with wide sliding doors at the entrance. Daisy was escorted inside by the female officer, still in handcuffs. A security guard stood inside the entrance and motioned them over to the desk. Buckley followed them in, but the DCI didn't get out of the car. He couldn't even look at her.

She signed in with the duty sergeant and was asked to hand over her coat. After that, she was taken to a holding cell until her legal representative arrived. At least they weren't allowed to interview her without Greg present.

Daisy didn't see DCI McGuinness again until she was led into the interview room almost an hour later. It was the same one as before with the steel table and cold-backed chairs. Greg was already there waiting for her, along with McGuinness and Buckley. She fell into his arms. "Oh, Greg. I don't understand what's going on!"

He hugged her, then told her to take a seat. McGuinness was watching her, his expression inscrutable. She knew he didn't for a minute believe she was capable of murder, but even she had to admit, the evidence was pretty compelling. DNA didn't lie. Somehow, she'd contaminated herself, and now she was in real trouble.

McGuinness introduced everyone for the purposes of the recording. He kept his voice low and steady, but

Daisy could tell by the muscles working in his jaw that he wasn't as composed as he pretended to be. Buckley sat beside him as he'd done before, straight-backed and stiff. There was a manila file in front of McGuinness on the table. Daisy recognised it as the Melanie Haverstock case file because it had a little doodle on it that she'd seen him draw the last time they were in this room together.

The questioning began. First up was how the victim's DNA came to be on her gloves and coat sleeves. Greg warned her that she didn't have to say anything that might incriminate her, but she forced a smile and told him, the tape, and the men seated opposite her that she had nothing to hide. The sooner they got to the bottom of this, the sooner she could go home, and they could concentrate on finding the real killer.

She'd given this question a lot of thought on the way there, after the initial shock at being arrested had worn off. "I think it must have been from earlier in the day," she said. "Melanie had a hair appointment that morning. I didn't tend to her myself, my head stylist did, but we spoke briefly before she left."

"What did you talk about?" DCI McGuinness leaned forward in his chair.

"She paid her bill, then we walked out together. I was going out for lunch, and she was leaving the salon."

"But did you actually touch her?" Daisy could hear the strain in his voice. He was looking for ways to exonerate her, she knew that; she only wished she could oblige.

Then she remembered, and her heart leaped into her throat. "Yes, yes, I did!"

They all gazed at her expectantly. "As we left the salon, Melanie tripped and I caught her. It was only a little stumble, which is why I didn't think of it before, but that must have been when her DNA got onto my gloves and coat."

"You were wearing them at the time?" McGuinness didn't look convinced.

"Yes, I was. I always put them on when I'm going out." She turned to Greg. "I knew there was a logical explanation."

"What kind of DNA was recovered?" the lawyer asked.

Good point. If it was blood, then her theory would go flying out of the window. She watched McGuinness's face, holding her breath.

It twitched, then he said, "Skin and hair fibres. No blood."

Phew. Daisy exhaled and sank back into her chair.

Greg nodded.

"Can anyone back up what you just told us?" asked DCI McGuinness.

Crap. Her heart plummeted again. "I don't know. I'm not sure if anyone saw her stumble. You could ask the others."

"Oh, I will, don't worry about that."

"Is there any CCTV in the area?" asked Greg.

Of course! If there was, that would prove that what she'd told them was the truth. Oh, she could hug Greg.

McGuinness was nodding. "I'll get on to the council."

"The newsagent across the road has a private camera outside his store. He installed it after a break-in a few weeks back," she blurted out.

Please let it have been operational on Saturday.

McGuinness perked up. "Would that cover the alley-way that leads to the back of your salon?"

She shook her head. "Unfortunately not. The entrance to the alleyway is farther down, next to the church. From what I can gather, Mr. Patel's camera covers the pavement outside his shop and the road, as well as my front door."

"And you know this how?" asked McGuinness.

"He told me when he bought the camera. He said he'd keep an eye on my place for me."

"And you only thought to tell me now?" He ran a hand through his hair, which left it sticking up in tufts.

Daisy shrugged. "I'm sorry. With everything that's happened, I completely forgot."

He shook his head, then turned to Buckley, who'd been scribbling on his notepad. "Get that camera feed ASAP. I want to see footage for the full twenty-four hours leading up to the murder." Buckley scrambled off his chair and darted out.

"DS Buckley has left the room," McGuinness stated for the tape.

Greg patted her hand. "This is positive, Daisy."

"Let's hope that camera feed backs up your statement," McGuinness said, his face less tense than it was a few minutes ago.

Daisy felt less tense too. "It will," she said, more confidently than she felt. "Oh, and while we're here, there is something else I'd like to share with you."

"Yes?" He looked worried again. Greg flashed her a concerned glance.

"I spoke to Yvette Bechard this morning—she owns the French boutique next door to my salon. Melanie Haverstock was tormenting her."

"What do you mean 'tormenting'?" The frown was back across McGuinness's forehead.

"The store was having financial difficulties, and Yvette was going to have to shut it down. Melanie knew this because her husband, Douglas Haverstock, is Yvette's accountant. Melanie was the one who informed Betting Direct about the state of Yvette's finances, and they in turn were pressuring her to sell. A man called Olaf was harassing her. I even saw him come out of the store this morning, and when I went in, Yvette was in floods of tears. She told me everything."

Buckley's pen had stopped scribbling. He didn't know what to make of this sudden change in direction.

McGuinness rubbed his forehead as if to smooth out the lines. "Are you saying that Yvette had a motive to kill Melanie Haverstock because . . . ?"

"Because Melanie told Betting Direct that the boutique was in financial trouble."

"That doesn't strike me as much of a motive. So what? Stores go bust all the time. It doesn't mean the owners resort to murder."

"No, but you have to understand the way Melanie operated. She was a bully. She would have enjoyed tormenting poor Yvette, who has been part of the community for ten years. Melanie is . . . was insanely jealous of anyone who had something she didn't, and Yvette had style and social standing, two things Melanie lacked. Besides, the pressure this Olaf character was putting on Yvette was intense. She was in pieces when I found her this morning."

There was a pause as the detectives processed this new information. Eventually, McGuinness said, "Okay, let's take a break." He turned off the recording.

Daisy heaved a sigh of relief, and Greg squeezed her hand. She knew then it was going to be okay.

"Tea?" asked McGuinness, glancing at them.

"Please," said Greg. Daisy nodded. McGuinness and Buckley left the room.

"He's going to check your theory of how the DNA was transferred," Greg told her. "It might take a while, and unfortunately you'll have to stay in the holding cell until they confirm it."

"Great," said Daisy, leaning back in her chair. "At least I get my own room."

Greg smiled. "You're doing great, Daisy. Hang in there. It'll all be over soon."

"How's Donna?" Daisy asked, desperate to talk about something else other than what she'd been through these last few hours. What she needed right now was normality.

"She's worried about you, of course. She was on the phone to Floria as I left."

"I'm sorry for dragging you out here. I didn't know who else to call."

"You did the right thing. I'm not a criminal attorney, but at least I can hold your hand through the process. If you were going to trial, we'd have to assign you someone else."

"It won't go to trial, though, will it?" Daisy felt a flicker of alarm.

"Unlikely, especially if they can find the CCTV evidence of Melanie tripping and you catching her."

Daisy ran a hand through her hair. "I hope it was recording that day, because if not . . ." It didn't bear thinking about.

"Let's stay positive," urged Greg.

"Yes, you're right." Daisy took a deep breath. "I wish I'd thought of it earlier. It might have saved us all this trouble."

"Doubtful," said Greg. "It would still have been your word against theirs. They'd have brought you in regardless."

McGuinness and Buckley came back with the tea. It was sweet, which was good. It would take the edge off her shock and give her some energy. As it was, she was fighting to keep her eyes open.

He switched the recording back on and reiterated what he'd said before, about who was present. "None of your staff remembers Melanie falling as she left the salon," he said, drumming his fingers on the table. "But we've requested the video footage from across the street. The owner says his camera is operational, so we should have something soon."

"Oh, thank goodness." Daisy clutched her teacup. It was going to be okay.

McGuinness studied her for a moment, then pulled a plastic bag out of his jacket pocket and put it on the table in front of him. "Did you receive more of these?" he asked.

Daisy recognised it. The two notes had been stuffed into her pocket along with her mobile phone and keys. They'd been taken off her when she'd been searched entering the police station.

"No." She hesitated. "One belongs to Yvette Bechard, and the other to Liz Roberts."

She avoided McGuinness's furrowed gaze.

"And you were going to tell me about these, when?"

Daisy grimaced. She'd really messed up. "I know, I'm sorry. I was going to tell you, but didn't get a chance before you arrested me. Yvette's note was hand delivered to the boutique, and Liz found hers in her post box this afternoon."

McGuinness scratched his head. "Liz Roberts? The lady whose husband is having an affair with Melanie Haverstock?"

Daisy nodded.

"Why do you have them?" asked McGuinness.

Daisy sighed. Liz was going to kill her, and Yvette didn't even know she had a letter yet. "Liz came into the salon in a panic this afternoon. She'd found the note and was adamant the person who sent it had done so because they knew about the affair and thought Liz had killed Melanie."

"We've cleared her from our investigation," said McGuinness, his expression stern.

"I know. She left the salon in an Uber the night of the murder and went straight home."

McGuinness didn't ask her how she knew that. He simply sighed and said, "Why did she bring it to you?"

Oh dear. He was going to love this one. "She wanted me to find out who sent it."

A flush crept into McGuinness's cheeks, and his steel gaze hardened. "You didn't think it was worth bringing this to my attention?"

"Liz begged me not to. She said you'd already interviewed her today, and she didn't want to go through that again. Besides, she was worried about her reputation. She doesn't want the community to know her husband was

sleeping with Melanie Haverstock, or that she's been ac-
cused of murder. The police aren't known for their discre-
tion, I'm afraid."

The muscle in the side of his jaw began to work.
"What about Yvette Bechard?"

"Well, I picked that up off her counter. It was with the
morning post. I'm not even sure she noticed it."

"You mean you took it without her knowing?" He
looked incredulous.

Daisy sighed. This was not going well.

He shook his head. "The investigation takes prece-
dence. You should have brought these to me immediately."

"I know. I'm sorry." Daisy glanced down at her hands.
He was right. She ought to have told him. Withholding
evidence in a police case was not something she was
proud of.

"I suppose your prints are on them, too, now?"

"I picked up Yvette's and Liz thrust hers into my hand.
What was I supposed to do?" Yes, she'd made a mistake,
but really, she had only been trying to help.

"I expected more of you, Daisy." His quiet disappoint-
ment irked her more than any chastisement. Especially
since she knew she was in the wrong.

"Did you find any prints on my note?" she asked in a
small voice.

"No."

Just then there was a knock on the interview room
door. McGuinness got up to answer it. A female officer
murmured something to him, and he nodded.

"This interview is terminated," he said abruptly from
the doorway. Then to Buckley, "Put Miss Thorne back
into the holding cell until we've verified her statement."

"What's happened?" asked Daisy, jumping out of her chair.

"There's been another incident," he told her, his eyes boring into hers.

"What?" she whispered.

"Your colleague, Penny, was attacked on her way home this evening."

Chapter Seventeen

"Oh my gosh, is she okay?" gasped Daisy. Penny had been attacked? Why? Her head spun as she tried to make sense of it. Who would want to harm her sweet-natured colleague? Penny didn't have a mean bone in her body.

McGuinness was curt. "She's been taken to the West Middlesex Hospital. That's all I know, sorry."

Daisy turned to Greg. "Will you find out for me? Please, Greg." She turned to McGuinness. "I should be there. I should be with her."

"You're still under arrest, Daisy. Until your story checks out, I'm afraid I can't release you."

"I'll send Donna over there right now," said Greg, pulling out his phone. "Floria can go with her. They'll find out all the details."

"Could you call Niall, as well? Floria will have his

number." Penny's boyfriend deserved to be told, and he was a wealthy, respected figure in the community. If any strings needed pulling, he was the man to do it.

Greg nodded. "Don't worry. I'll take care of it, and I'll wait in reception until you're cleared to go home."

"Thanks, Greg." Daisy hugged him, then let Buckley lead her away. This was turning into one of the worst days ever. Threatening notes. Being arrested. And now Penny had been attacked. What else could go wrong?

Buckley took her back to the holding cell. "I'm sorry to have to do this, ma'am," he said as she walked inside and sat down on the bench. "Let me know if you need anything."

"I'll be fine, Sergeant."

"My apologies again, ma'am." He looked so awkward standing in the doorway. "You shouldn't be treated this way."

"That's okay," she said, giving him a weak smile. "It's the way things go. Just check that camera footage and get me out of here as soon as possible."

He nodded. "Yes, ma'am." And he closed the door, locking it behind him.

Despite it being the middle of the night, it didn't take long for the newsagent across the street from Ooh La La to supply the video footage of the afternoon in question. That was one of the benefits of living above the store. He was only too happy that his new purchase had come in handy, and even more so that it had gotten Daisy off the hook.

There it was, clear as day. Melanie Haverstock took a tumble outside the store, and Daisy had caught her—just as she'd said. The woman's hands had been all over Daisy's coat sleeves. That was what Buckley told her when he'd released her sometime later. In addition, Daisy had been in custody when Penny was attacked, which meant she couldn't be the perpetrator, assuming that it was the same person who'd killed Melanie.

It was now nearly midnight, too late to visit Penny at the hospital, but Greg gave her a full update. "She was walking home when her assailant crept up behind her and hit her over the head. Penny went down immediately; she never saw her attacker. Luckily, she's got a hard head, and while she's concussed, she's not in any serious danger. Donna said they're keeping her in overnight as a precaution."

"Thank God," breathed Daisy, as Greg sped along the motorway towards Edgemead. "Do they know what she was hit with?"

"They think it was a brick. There was red concrete in the wound."

"She's lucky to be alive," murmured Daisy.

"Do you think this is connected to the investigation?" asked Greg, flicking his high beams on as the road opened up in front of them. The scenery on either side was becoming way too familiar. Daisy would be quite happy if she never had to travel this road again.

"It must be," said Daisy. "Otherwise it's a hell of a co-incidence."

"Hmm . . ." muttered Greg, dimming his brights as another vehicle approached. "I was afraid you'd say that."

"I'll go and stay with Floria and Josh," Daisy said as they turned off the motorway towards Edgemead. "There are too many weird things going on at the moment."

"I think that's probably a good idea," Greg agreed. "Shall I drop you there now?"

"Oh no. Tomorrow will be soon enough. I want to go

home and take a shower. I've been in a cell for the last four hours."

Greg chuckled. "I'm glad that was cleared up so easily. I have to admit, I was quite concerned when I got to the station. I wasn't sure how you were going to get out of that one."

"I've been in a few scrapes before," Daisy admitted, "but I've never been arrested. It's not an experience I want to repeat."

"I don't think Paul thought for a moment that you were responsible, if it's any consolation." He gave her a sideways glance. "He's a good man, Daisy. He was just doing his job."

"I know."

"The evidence was fairly incriminating."

It was. She'd had a lucky escape. From now on, she'd be very careful whom she talked to and where she poked her nose. No more favours for friends, no more failing to disclose evidence. From now on, she was going to play it by the book. Her brush with the law had made her realise that this detecting business was no joke. It had to be taken seriously, or there were consequences.

"I suppose, on the bright side, it does give me added insight into the criminal justice system for my criminology diploma."

Greg laughed. "Only you could turn getting arrested into a positive."

Greg dropped her off, and as Daisy let herself in, she thought she'd never been so grateful to be home. After a long, hot shower where she scrubbed every inch of her body until it was red and glowing, she collapsed into bed. Her eyes were closed almost before her head hit the pillow.

A loud ringing sound penetrated her subconscious.

She groaned. Seriously? She propped herself up on her elbow and glanced at her mobile phone, which was plugged in beside her. Four a.m. She'd only been asleep for three hours.

"What the . . . ?"

It was a withheld number. Her first thought was that something had happened to Penny, and her heart began beating frantically.

"Hello?" she answered, her voice thick with tiredness and trepidation.

"Is that Miss Daisy Thorne?" said an official, female voice.

"Yes, who is this?"

"This is Sergeant Angela Basset from the Surbiton Police Department. We have a Krish Ranga . . . Ranganathan here who wants to talk to you." She stumbled over his surname.

"Put him through." What was Krish doing at the police department at this time of night? She didn't have to wait long to find out as Krish's voice came on the line.

"Daisy. Oh Daisy." He burst into tears, and Daisy could hear him sobbing at the other end of the line.

"What's wrong?" she demanded but didn't get a reply.

"Krish, what's happened?" Her pulse was racing. All this trauma was wreaking havoc on her nerves. It must be something dreadful to reduce the normally chirpy Krish to this blubbering mess.

The female officer came back on the line. "Mr. Ranganathan is asking if you'll come down to the police station, ma'am. His boyfriend, Ross Monroe, was stabbed and killed tonight."

For a moment Daisy couldn't compute. Ross? She

stared at a speck on the bedroom wall until it blurred in front of her eyes, then she got it. Ross was Krish's new boyfriend, the hot, young rugby player with the reassuring thighs.

"Oh gosh. Yes, of course. I'll come as soon as I can."

Stabbed?

First Melanie. Then Penny. Now Ross. What the hell was going on? Daisy sat up and switched on the bedside lamp. Her gritty, tired eyes took a moment to adjust. Were they connected? She wasn't a great believer in coincidences. But how? Why? The questions flitted through her mind, but there were no answers. Before she got out of bed, she called DCI McGuinness.

"Haven't you had enough of me for one night?" McGuinness grumbled when he answered the phone. His voice was groggy, and the Irish lilt was more pronounced. Like her, he must have only had a few hours' sleep.

"There's been another murder," she blurted out.

Instantly, his tone changed. "Who? Where? Are you alright?"

Touched by his concern, she elaborated, "I'm fine. It's Krish's boyfriend, Ross. He was stabbed tonight in Surbiton. Krish just called me from the police station. He's in bits."

"How did it happen?" McGuinness barked, fully awake now.

"I don't know yet. I was about to go down there to collect him, but I thought I'd let you know first."

"I'll call them right away. Appreciate the heads-up."

He hung up, and Daisy heaved her heavy, protesting limbs out of bed. Crumbs, she really needed to get some decent shut-eye or she'd be a zombie before long. At least she'd informed McGuinness, so he couldn't moan at her for withholding evidence anymore.

She got dressed, washed her face, and climbed into her Volkswagen. The streets were empty this time of night, or rather morning, and she made it to the Surbiton Police Station in under half an hour. Krish was sitting in the lobby, a can of Coke from the vending machine next to him, his eyes red and swollen from sobbing. Daisy went straight over to him and gave him a hug.

"Krish, what on earth happened?"

He shook his head against her shoulder and clung to her for a long moment. She felt him shudder, then he glanced up. His eyes were hollow and empty. "We went to a bar in Surbiton and were walking home when I popped into a newsagent for some ciggies. I was paying when I heard this terrible yell from outside. I ran out to see Ross lying on the ground, blood pouring from two wounds in his lower back. Someone in a hoodie had run up and stabbed him."

She took his hand. "Oh Krish. That's awful. Did they catch him?"

Krish shook his head. "No, it happened so fast. The guy was long gone before the police arrived."

"I'm so sorry."

"Why would anyone want to hurt Ross?" Krish murmured, gazing down at his lap. Daisy had never seen him so dejected before. Her heart went out to him.

"I don't know," she whispered. It did seem senseless. Unless . . . "Maybe he didn't intend to. The attacker could have been after you, but he got the wrong guy."

Krish glanced up, his eyes wide. "Me? Why on earth would someone want to stab me? I'm just a gay hairdresser, for Christ's sake. I don't have enemies, other than my parents, of course, who still aren't talking to me, but I don't think they'd resort to murder."

"I don't know." Daisy patted his hand and masked a small smile. Krish's relationship with his parents was difficult, but he could still make light of it. It was his way of coping with the fact they'd disowned him. "After Melanie's death outside the salon and what happened to Penny earlier this evening, I wonder if this could be connected."

"What happened to Penny?" He glanced up.

Daisy instantly regretted her words. Krish had enough to deal with without worrying about Penny. Tiredness had fuddled her brain. She ought to have kept that to herself until tomorrow morning, when he'd be better able to process it.

"Tell me, Daisy," he insisted, his gaze filled with concern. "Is Penny okay?"

"She's was attacked," Daisy said with a reluctant sigh. "On her way home from work this evening. She's in hospital."

Krish's eyes grew huge and he opened his mouth to say something, but Daisy held up her hand. "But the doctors say she's going to be fine. It's just a concussion."

"Oh, thank goodness." He leaned back against the black, plastic chair and shut his eyes. She could see faint purple shadows beneath them, and his skin was sallow and wan. Like her, he desperately needed sleep.

"What the hell is going on, Daisy?" he asked, opening his eyes and staring up at the ceiling. "Do you think the guy who stabbed Ross is the same person who killed Melanie?"

"It's crossed my mind, yes." She sighed and gave a little shrug. "But I could be wrong. You and Ross don't look anything alike." Ross was six foot tall with a muscular physique, whereas Krish was slender and Asian. There was no way the killer could have mistaken the one for the other.

"No, we don't." His lip quivered, and she knew he was thinking about his friend, who'd been killed right in front of him.

"Was he mugged?" she asked suddenly. Krish hadn't given her any details of the attack. Maybe this was a mugging gone wrong, an unrelated event—and any connection was a product of her exhausted, overactive imagination. Was she seeing patterns where none existed? It was quite possible, given the lack of sleep and strain of the last twenty-four hours.

He shook his head. "I don't think so. The attacker ran away as soon as I came out of the shop."

"You saw him?" Daisy exclaimed.

"From the back. He was tall—almost as tall as Ross—and wore a hoodie. I didn't see his face."

"Build? Running stance? Anything else you noticed about him?" Daisy knew it was important to question witnesses as soon as possible after the crime, because once some time had passed, their memory wasn't as reliable.

"Slim build," Krish said, his face contorted with the effort of remembering the traumatic event. He shook his head. "I'm sorry, I didn't notice anything else. I was too busy tending to Ross." He sniffed. "He died on the way to hospital."

"I'm so sorry, Krish." Daisy hugged him again. He rested his head on her shoulder but didn't cry.

"I didn't know him that well," Krish mumbled into her shoulder. "But I really liked him. He wasn't even gay, you know. We were taking it slow."

"Shh . . ." Daisy stroked his back. She felt all the energy drain out of him. He was exhausted.

"Come on," she said, after a long moment had passed. "Let's get out of here."

He nodded, and let Daisy lead him to her car. They didn't talk on the way home. Daisy was lost in thought, and Krish stared out of the window, a look of utter desolation on his normally happy face. Daisy drove him back to her place and made up the sleeper couch. He shouldn't be alone tonight. After she'd tucked him up, she stumbled upstairs to bed. Her brain was too exhausted to process the events of the night. Right now, sleep was all she could think about. Tomorrow she'd contemplate what had happened and try to make some sense out of it. Tomorrow would be soon enough.

Chapter Eighteen

Daisy came downstairs to the delicious aroma of fried eggs and bacon, and strong home-brewed coffee. Krish had been busy. His mood was much improved, and he was humming away to the radio as he cooked.

"That smells wonderful," Daisy said, her stomach rumbling in agreement.

"I thought we could use a good fry-up." He gestured for her to take a seat at the bar counter that divided the kitchen from the lounge and served as an impromptu dining room table. On it, he'd placed a pot of coffee and two mugs. His was half full. "Then maybe we can visit Pen?"

She reached for the coffee. "I want to see her, too."

Krish turned his back on the sizzling bacon. "You said it was a concussion, right? She's going to be okay? 'Cause I couldn't bear it if anything happened to Pen."

They'd become very close working together over the last few years.

Daisy gave a slim smile. "Yes, luckily she has a hard head."

He nodded and turned back to the stove. "So, what actually happened?"

Daisy poured herself a cup of coffee. She felt much better than yesterday—that overpowering weariness had lifted—but she couldn't operate on full cylinders until she'd had her morning caffeine fix. After she'd taken a few big sips, she glanced up at Krish, who was putting the eggs onto two plates. "According to Greg, she was walking to the bus station just after six o'clock when someone snuck up behind her and hit her on the head with a brick. That's all we know."

"In the high street?" He turned around, spatula poised in midair.

"No, in the alley next to the churchyard, but still, it's a popular shortcut to the high street. You'd think someone would have seen something."

Krish shrugged. "It would have been dark at that time. Did Penny see her attacker?"

"No, she was knocked out cold and woke up lying on the pavement surrounded by paramedics."

"Crikey." He placed the bacon onto the plates and then the toast popped up.

Daisy tapped her fingertips on the counter. "I called Asa this morning and told her to close the hair salon until noon."

At his look of alarm, she said, "You're in no condition to work, and with Penny in hospital we're short-staffed. I've got Asa rescheduling everybody's appointments."

Krish handed her a plate and they ate, the food restoring their spirits and energy. When they were nearly done, Daisy said, "First Melanie was killed, then Penny was attacked, and now Ross has been stabbed. What did they all know that made them a target?" She frowned at Krish. "There must be a link between them, but for the life of me, I can't figure out what it is."

"So, we're assuming they're connected?" He put down his knife and fork.

"Yes. It's too much of a coincidence, otherwise. Three attacks in a week. They must be related."

He gazed at her with his big, brown puppy-dog eyes. "I can't see how Ross is related to any of this. He didn't know Melanie, or anyone else for that matter. I met him at the rugby club."

"That's true," she admitted. "Which is why I thought maybe the killer meant to go for you but got Ross instead." She ran a hand through her hair. "Except that doesn't make sense, either, since you're so different. Even at night it would be impossible to mistake the big rugby player for you."

Krish's face fell.

"No offense," Daisy added.

He shook his head. "No, it's fine. Ross was so wonderfully tall and broad. I couldn't believe it when he agreed to go out with me. I can't believe he's gone." A sob caught in his throat. Daisy reached across the counter and squeezed his hand.

There was a lull in the conversation as Krish cleared up the plates and loaded the dishwasher, and Daisy finished her coffee. Now that she was nourished and her neurons had been kick-started, a thought was playing at the edge of her mind. "Unless they didn't know who you were and took a guess," she said, putting down her mug. "But they got the wrong guy."

"Why would anyone want to kill me?" Krish pointed to himself with a fork.

"That's an excellent question," she said. "For that matter, why would anyone want to hit Penny on the head?"

He fell silent. "Maybe they thought we'd seen something?"

Daisy nodded. That had been her thought, too, although it seemed a fairly extreme action for a hunch. Quite clearly, neither Pen nor Krish knew anything about Melanie's murder, or who the perpetrator was.

"One thing we can be sure of is this series of attacks has got to do with Melanie, somehow. She was the one it all started with. The first victim."

They finished the pot of coffee, and Daisy washed up the few bits and pieces that didn't go in the dishwasher. "I can't see a connection," she eventually said, wiping her hands on the tea towel. "We must be missing something."

None the wiser, they decided to get dressed and go to visit Penny. The busy university hospital was situated in Isleworth, a cosmopolitan west London suburb twenty minutes from Edgemead. The reception was buzzing, and it took Daisy and Krish twenty minutes to find out which ward Penny was in. Zone E, ward five. They set off in the direction the harried receptionist had indicated, down a long corridor with pale lime-green walls that made Daisy feel like she was underwater. A lingering smell of antiseptic and trepidation hung in the air.

"I hate hospitals," Krish muttered, picking up the pace. They rounded a corner, walked down another long passage, then turned another corner into a lobby, this time with pale yellow paint on the walls. At least it was a bit cheerier than the green. An elevator took them up three floors to the wards.

They asked a sister at the nurses' station which room Penny was in and were taken to a large ward with five patients in identical metal-framed beds all situated next to each other in a neat row. Two were sleeping, one was reading a book, and the other was sitting up knitting. There was no privacy, other than the white curtains that could be drawn around the beds, but which were currently all open and pinned back against the wall.

Penny looked pale and fragile against the white hospital sheets, propped up by numerous bulky pillows. There was a large bandage around her head where she'd been hit with the brick.

"Hi, darling," sang Krish, as he walked in brandishing an enormous bunch of helium balloons that he'd bought from the downstairs gift shop. "How are you feeling?"

She broke into a weak smile as she saw them. "I'm okay. Gosh, thanks for the balloons. You must have bought out the entire shop. Where am I going to put them?"

"Right here," said Krish, tying them to the foot of the bed. The two other patients who were awake looked over in astonishment.

"Any more and she'll lift off," Daisy warned with a grin. "Hi, Pen." She leaned over and gave her colleague and friend a gentle hug. "How are you feeling?"

Penny grimaced. "My head hurts, but otherwise okay. They tell me I'll live. More importantly, how are you? I heard you escaped."

Daisy laughed. "McGuinness let me go. They realised

the DNA on my gloves and coat were from an encounter with Melanie earlier in the day. It was all a big misunderstanding."

"I'm so pleased. I was terribly worried. Floria said Greg was wonderful."

"He was," Daisy agreed. "I don't know what I would have done without him."

Penny grasped Krish's hand. "I'm so sorry about Ross. Are you okay?"

"I will be," he said, his eyes clouding over. "Ross was a lovely guy. I miss him."

"I'm sure you do. Were you two close?"

"We were getting there," admitted Krish, closing his eyes briefly as if to try to shut out the memory.

"What a terrible thing to happen. Do they know who did it?"

"The Surbiton police are treating it as a knife crime incident," said Daisy, rolling her eyes. "But I don't believe that for a second."

"It does seem to be a weird coincidence," mused Penny. "But why would our killer target Ross?"

"For the same reason they targeted you," Daisy said, voicing her theory. "They think you know something."

"But I don't." Penny shook her head, then winced. "It doesn't make any sense."

Daisy sighed. She was right. None of this made sense. "Perhaps the killer thought you saw something the night of Mel's murder," she suggested, although it didn't seem right. "You left early. Perhaps they thought you spotted them waiting in the shadows."

Penny frowned. "It was raining when I left. I dashed to the bus stop and got on almost immediately. I didn't pass anyone I knew."

"It's just an idea. I'm grasping at straws here. And why Ross? What did he know?"

They both turned to Krish, who shifted awkwardly on the bed.

"Krish?" asked Daisy, as a thought struck her. "Have you been blabbing to Ross about the investigation?"

He threw up his hands. "Now, Daisy, don't get mad . . . but I may have told him about our suspects," he said sheepishly.

Daisy stared at him. "Krish! Why didn't you mention this before?"

"I forgot. But what does it matter? He still doesn't know anyone, so he can't be involved."

"What exactly did you tell him?" whispered Daisy. The lady in the bed next to Penny's was pretending not to listen while her knitting needles tapped furiously together. Daisy got up and pulled the curtain closed around the bed. It became very crowded in their little cubicle with the three of them and the multitude of colourful balloons swaying above their heads.

Krish hung his head and spoke quietly. "I told him we were investigating the murder of a customer. I told him what had happened, and he was intrigued. He wanted to know more about it, said he was an Agatha Christie fan and loved murder mysteries."

"So you indulged him?" Daisy shook her head.

Krish gave a miserable nod. "Yes, I told him about our suspects, and how the police had questioned all of us at the salon."

"Did you mention names?" Daisy asked, her gaze fixed on him.

"He was so interested. I didn't think it would matter. They were just names, he doesn't know who they are."

"But he could find out," murmured Daisy.

Penny stared at them both. "Do you think this information is what got him killed?"

"No." Krish shook his head. "I told you, he didn't know anyone. He wasn't involved."

Daisy sighed. "How do you know that, Krish? He could have told someone, and by some twist of fate, they just happened to be the killer. That could be why he was silenced."

"Do you think so?" whispered Penny, who'd gone even whiter.

"It's the only explanation that makes sense. Why else would he have been attacked? The only connection he had to this case was you, Krish."

"Oh no . . ." Krish put a hand over his mouth. "This is my fault, isn't it? Me and my big mouth. I'm the reason Ross is dead." He pushed himself off the bed, flung back the curtain, and ran from the room.

Daisy immediately felt bad. "Damn it. I know that was a bit harsh, but honestly, Krish has got to learn when to keep his mouth shut."

"He can't help himself," Penny whispered. "It's just the way he is."

Daisy got up off the bed. "I'd better go after him."

Penny touched her arm. "Give him a minute to calm down. I want to tell you what I found out at Yvette's."

Heavens, with everything that had happened, Daisy had forgotten that Penny was going to visit Yvette after work to try to find out her movements on Saturday night. "Of course! Tell me, did you discover her alibi?"

"Sort of," Penny said. "Yvette spent Saturday evening in central London. She went to the Fashion Through the Ages exhibition at the V&A Museum, then did some shopping in Oxford Street before taking the train back to Edgemead around ten-ish."

"If she can prove it, that puts her in the clear. Was she with anyone?"

"That's just it." Penny looked crestfallen. "She was alone. Although she showed me some photographs of the exhibition. There's no doubt she was there."

"But not necessarily Saturday evening," mused Daisy.

Penny shook her head. "Unless the phone time-stamps them."

That was a point. Most smartphones these days would have a time stamp on the pictures. That might be her saving grace.

"How did she seem?" asked Daisy. "Was she still upset about Olaf's visit, or anxious about the pending closure?"

"Yes, both of those things," Penny confirmed. "She said she wished there was some way she could save the boutique, but . . ." She shrugged. "I don't think there is. Yvette doesn't have any family who can help her out, and she's already remortgaged her apartment. This is the end of the line for her. It's so sad."

Yes, it was. Yvette's boutique had been a feature on the high street for a decade. It would be a shame to see it go, and Yvette along with it.

"Let me go and find Krish," said Daisy. "I think he's wallowed enough."

She found him sitting in the waiting area, his head in his hands. "I can't believe it," he kept saying. "This is all my fault."

"I'm sorry, Krish." Daisy sat down beside him. "I didn't mean to upset you. I'm just trying to figure out what happened to Ross, and I can't think of another reason why he'd be targeted, unless he'd had some contact with the killer."

Krish sniffed. "No, Daisy. You're right. I shouldn't have told him about our investigation. It was wrong of me. It's just that he was so curious. We talked about it for ages. I didn't realise he was so interested in mysteries. It was something we had in common, you know?"

"I know," she said kindly, patting his hand. "Come back to the ward, and we'll talk this through together and see if we can figure out what happened."

He trailed her back to Penny's room like a naughty puppy, his head bowed. If he had a tail, it would be between his legs right now. Penny patted the bed next to her, and he sat down. "I feel terrible."

"It's not your fault." Penny leaned forward and gave him a hug. "You weren't the one who stabbed him. You couldn't have known it would come to this."

Penny was right. Krish was just being . . . well, Krish. He wasn't the one who had wielded the knife. "Krish, think carefully, whom might Ross have told?" Daisy asked him. "Did he mention anyone to you? Any of our suspects whom he might have been in contact with?"

He frowned. "I don't know. He could have told any of his teammates or work colleagues." He shrugged. "It's hard to say. We didn't know the same people."

"He didn't mention anybody on our suspect list?" Daisy asked again. "Anyone who came into the salon that day?"

Krish ran a hand through his hair. "No, he didn't. I would have picked up on that."

Daisy blew a stray hair out of her face. Okay, they had to start thinking creatively. "Who goes to the rugby club that also knows Melanie Haverstock?" she asked, thinking that if they cross-referenced the two groups, they might come up with a common factor.

"The chairman, Bob Newman, and Roy Roberts, Liz's husband, of course. I can't think of anyone else, but I don't often hang out there. I only went because of Ross." He teared up again. Penny handed him a tissue from a box on her bed stand.

He was right, there were too many variables. It was impossible to know how many people at the rugby club knew Melanie. Could they assume the killer was someone there?

"Roy Roberts was having an affair with Melanie," she mused.

"Yes, but he didn't come into the salon that day," Penny pointed out. "He wouldn't have had access to your scissors."

"No, and Liz said he commutes to London every day. I think we can discount him."

"Same with the chairman," said Krish. "He's retired, but he doesn't need a hairdresser. He's completely bald."

"Where did Ross work?" Daisy asked.

"He was in banking and worked in the city. I never met any of his colleagues. Like I said, he wasn't gay. Not really. He wouldn't have wanted them to know about me."

Daisy nodded. "I'm pretty sure we can rule them out, then." The probability of someone at the city bank where Ross worked knowing Melanie Haverstock from their little village in Surrey was remote. Not entirely impossible, but extremely unlikely. As far as Daisy knew, Mel had never worked in the banking sector, and her husband was an introverted village accountant.

"I've got an idea," said Krish suddenly.

They all glanced up.

He gave a mischievous grin. "What if we took a look around Ross's flat? There might be a clue there as to whom he was talking to."

Daisy and Penny stared at him, then Penny whispered, "You mean, break in?"

Daisy bit her lip as the silence dragged out.

Krish shrugged. "It was just an idea."

"No, it's a good one," said Daisy.

Penny gasped. "Daisy, no. You can't seriously be considering this! What if you get caught? You could go to jail for real, this time."

She didn't want to think about that. Breaking and entering was a criminal offense, yet what if the clue to the killer lay inside Ross's apartment? Curiosity wrestled with her better judgement.

"I know, Pen, but Krish is right. It might shed some light onto whom Ross was talking to. It could help us find the killer."

Penny shook her head. "I don't like it. It's too dangerous."

"It might be the only way. If we don't find the killer, they could come back and try again."

She paled. "Have another crack at me, you mean?"

Daisy nodded. "None of us is safe. If Ross did speak to the murderer, they know we're investigating this crime, and there are only so many suspects on our list. It has to be someone who came into the salon on Saturday."

Penny thought about this for a moment, then she whispered, "How would you get in?"

"There's a bay window at the back with a faulty catch," Krish said, keeping his voice low. "Ross mentioned it once before when he was locking up. We might be able to force it."

"Let's give it a go," Daisy said, curiosity winning out. They didn't have any other leads to go on.

Krish jumped up. "We could go now. It's the middle of the day, most people will be at work."

"I don't like this," Penny murmured, an anxious frown on her face. "If DCI McGuinness finds out . . ."

"He's not going to find out," whispered Daisy. "We'll be in and out before anyone notices." She didn't want to think about what would happen if someone saw them. She turned back to Krish. "Where does Ross live?"

"Esher," said Krish. "But their rugby team is rubbish, so he played for Edgemead instead."

Daisy got to her feet. It was risky, there was no doubt about it, but how else were they going to find out whom Ross had spoken to? It could lead them directly to the killer. "Okay. Let's do it."

She hoped she wasn't going to regret this decision.

Chapter Nineteen

Ross lived in a small, neat apartment block in Esher behind the station. Daisy parked two blocks away near the
train tracks, so no one would connect them with the
break-in, and they proceeded on foot to the property. As
they got closer, Daisy nudged Krish and glanced upwards. An old lady with white hair had parted the curtains
and was staring down into the street below. "Keep walking," she muttered.

They passed the block, then double-backed around the
rear, out of sight of the front windows. Daisy studied the
back of the building. The windows were smaller on this
side, and some were made of dimpled glass, probably
bathrooms and kitchens. As far as she could see, no shadowy figures were looking out. They were in the clear.

A low brick wall surrounded the property, against

which a thick hedge grew. The hedge extended above the wall, providing a foot of extra coverage, which would come in handy if anyone walked past on the street. This was a sleepy suburban area with few cars and little foot traffic. What there was, was mostly young mothers with prams or retired folk walking up to the small parade of shops a few streets away.

Daisy and Krish entered through a flimsy garden gate that spanned a gap in the brick wall. It was in good condition, made of wrought iron and freshly painted, but it was unlocked. So far, no breaking. Just entering.

"Great security," murmured Daisy, as they shut it behind them with a soft click.

"Ouch," hissed Krish as he caught his arm on a rosebush that had managed to intertwine itself with the hedge. Random branches stuck out in all directions, their sharp, jagged thorns waiting to catch unsuspecting visitors by surprise.

Daisy turned around. "Don't leave any evidence behind," she whispered.

Krish raised an eyebrow but stopped and inspected the branch. "All clear," he murmured. No threads or fibres had been left on the thorny bush.

They moved forwards around the back of the block to the far side, Krish taking the lead.

"It's over here." He pointed to a large bay window whilst crouching behind the hedgerows. Daisy followed, keeping her head down and an eye out for walkers-by. The window faced onto the communal washing line and a small patch of lawn rimmed with neatly pruned plants. Somebody cared enough to tend to this garden.

"Here, put these on." Daisy pulled a pair of blue latex gloves out of her pocket and handed them to him.

His eyes widened. "Where did you get these?"

"I took them from the nurses' station at the hospital," she replied. There was no sense in leaving fingerprints all over the place. She'd had enough run-ins with the law to last her a lifetime, thanks very much.

Krish pulled them on, a look of bewilderment on his face. "I can't believe you thought of this. It's so . . . it's so . . ."

"Clever?" Daisy suggested.

"Premeditated," he finished.

She grinned. "This was your idea."

He grimaced. "Don't remind me."

Krish put his hands on the bottom frame of the window and pushed. It didn't move.

"Can you open it?" Daisy peered around them, checking the perimeter. So far, so good. The apartment next door was in darkness, and they were too close to the wall for anyone upstairs to see them, unless they peered vertically down out of the window. The peeping granny was around the other side, and the neighbouring house was surrounded by rapidly shedding oak trees that still had enough foliage on them to obscure any view.

Krish gave it a firm heave, but it didn't budge.

Daisy glanced at him in alarm. "Try again."

He wiggled it, rattling the frame. Then he tried lifting it again, and this time it opened a crack.

Yes! They were in.

Krish lifted the window far enough so that they could crawl through. Daisy went first, lifting her leg over the sill and hoisting herself up onto the ledge. She ducked through the small space, then brought her other leg over, before landing awkwardly on the floor on the inside.

Just then, they heard footsteps on the cement path that

led around the building to the washing line. An elderly voice rang out. "I don't know why I bother. Nothing ever dries in this weather."

"At least it's not raining, Joyce," said another.

Krish dove headfirst through the open window. He landed hard in a heap on the floor, attempted an army roll, and knocked over a potted Delicious Monster.

It toppled over and the ceramic pot cracked, but luckily the soil was so netted by the root system that it held together and didn't spill out over the floor.

"Watch out," hissed Daisy, straightening the potted plant, trying to avoid the massive leaves. "We don't want to trash the place." Or leave any trace evidence.

"Ross won't care," said Krish, getting to his feet. He gazed around the flat with sad eyes. "That plant will probably die now."

Daisy patted his shoulder in sympathy, then straightened up and looked around. The living room was sparsely furnished with items that no young man would have bought for himself. She guessed they'd been donated by his parents. A worn leather sofa, a mismatched armchair that had seen better days, and a ring-stained wooden coffee table in the centre of the room. Apart from the enormous flat-screen television, there were no pictures on the walls or other memorabilia. It was a typical guy's flat.

They walked into the hallway, and Daisy noticed a spare set of keys on the console table in front of the door. Beneath it was a shoe stand that contained mainly trainers and rugby boots. Krish came to a halt. "It's so sad to think that he's not around to wear them anymore."

Daisy squeezed his arm. "How many bedrooms?" she asked.

"Two," said Krish. "He uses the one as a study."

"You take the bedroom, I'll take the study."

He dragged his gaze away from the shoe rack and disappeared down the darkened hallway. Daisy turned left and entered a box-size room with a small window and a desk. The blinds were up and natural winter sunlight extended into the room, but it was too dark to effectively inspect nooks and crannies. She made a mental note to bring a torch next time she did anything like this. Actually, what was she thinking? There wouldn't be a next time. She wasn't going to make breaking and entering a habit.

Ross was surprisingly neat for a hulking, mud-covered, six-foot-plus rugby player. His shiny closed laptop lay in the centre of the desk beside a mousepad with the London Stock Exchange logo on it. Daisy ignored the device; it would be password-protected anyway. Ross was a banker. He would be security-conscious. She sifted through a small pile of papers on the one side, mostly overdue bills and outstanding council tax notices, and a reminder to register to vote. Nothing of interest there.

She turned her attention to the three drawers that were positioned down the right-hand side of the desk. The top drawer contained stationery items, a hole punch, a stapler, and an assortment of paper clips, staples, and drawing pins in a used jam jar.

The second drawer contained printer paper and some plastic sheets, but it was the third drawer where she hit pay dirt.

Daisy stared at the contents for a long time, then she called to Krish, "You'd better come and have a look at this."

He walked into the room. "What?"

Daisy indicated the open drawer.

He peered in and then up at Daisy. "So? It's a notepad and a couple of marker pens."

Of course. Krish didn't know about the threatening "murderer" notes. She filled him in as she inspected the contents of drawer three more closely, taking each item out and studying it before replacing it into the exact same position as before. A white, unlined notepad, the exact size and texture as the notes, right down to the faded watermark in the top right corner, and two black felt-tipped pens of precisely the right thickness.

"No way," said Krish, when she'd finished her story. "I can't believe Ross would do something like that!"

"The proof is right here." She pointed to the items in the drawer. "It's a match."

"But why? What was he playing at?" Krish had turned ashen.

Daisy hesitated. "I'm not sure, but we have to tell McGuinness about this."

"We can't." Krish was appalled. "He'll know we were snooping, and then we'll be arrested."

Hmm. Good point. They couldn't exactly confess to breaking and entering. How else could she get the detective chief inspector to search Ross's apartment? Clearly the Surbiton police weren't going to since they thought it was just a random attack, and even if they did, the relevance of the notepad and marker pens would be lost on them.

She scratched her head. "We'll have to think of a way to tell him without incriminating ourselves." Then she remembered the extra key on the console table. "We can say Ross gave you a spare key."

"Will he believe that?" Krish looked doubtful.

"I don't see why not. It's plausible, right? You guys

were an item. It would stand to reason that he'd give you a key to his apartment."

"We weren't anywhere near that stage yet," murmured Krish.

"It doesn't matter. Who's going to know? It's one way of getting us off the hook and getting McGuinness in here with a search warrant." Daisy took a photograph of the contents of the drawer with the camera on her phone and then shut it again.

They were just leaving the study when there was a knock at the door. They froze and stared at each other. *Shit*, mouthed Krish.

Daisy tiptoed forward and peered through the peephole. It was a middle-aged man with greying hair and from this aspect, an enormous nose.

"Who is it?" whispered Krish.

Daisy shrugged. *No idea*, she mouthed back.

Another knock. Harder this time. Then a gravelly voice called, "Hello? This is the caretaker. Is there anyone in there?"

Crap! Someone must have seen them climb in. She bet it was that nosy old lady. Krish was flapping his arms in a panic like he was trying to take off. They heard the telltale jingle of keys as the caretaker prepared to let himself in.

Daisy grabbed the keys off the console table and thrust them at Krish. "Tell him you're Ross's boyfriend and you're here to pick up some personal items. Make it believable."

She ducked back into the living room and hid behind the faded leather sofa. With a bit of luck, the caretaker would believe Krish's story and not search the place. It was imperative she wasn't caught sneaking around a dead man's flat. A shiver went through her as an image of the interrogation room at the police station flashed through her mind. No way was she going back there!

"Coming," Krish called in his singsong voice and opened the front door.

Daisy held her breath.

"Can I help you?" the hairstylist asked politely.

There was a surprised pause, then the gravelly voice demanded, "Who are you?"

"Oh, I'm Ross's boyfriend, Krish. I don't believe we've met." He put on his campiest voice, and Daisy could imagine him flicking his wrist at the caretaker. Krish wasn't overtly gay, but he knew how to put it on when the situation required it. She bit her lip.

"I'm sorry? Did you say 'boyfriend'?" She could hear the confusion in his voice. For anyone who knew Ross, it would come as a surprise that the hulking centre-forward was a homosexual.

"Yeah, didn't you know?" He gave a soft chuckle. "Well, isn't that just like Ross to keep everyone in the dark."

"Oh, um . . . no, I didn't. What are you doing in his flat?"

Krish's tone turned sad. "I'm fetching some of the personal items I left here the weekend before Ross . . . well, you know . . ."

"Erm, yes. I was sorry to hear about his passing."

"It was so tragic," said Krish, a catch to his voice that Daisy suspected was real. "I was with him at the time, you know. One minute we were talking and laughing, the next he was lying on the pavement bleeding out." There was a muffled sniffle.

"I'm very sorry for your loss," the caretaker said.

Krish sniffed. "Thank you."

There was a pause, then he said, "I take it you have a key?"

"Yes." Daisy heard a jangle.

"Right, then." The caretaker cleared his throat. "I'll leave you to get on with it."

"Thank you."

A few seconds passed, then Daisy heard Krish say, "Do you mind if I take the potted plant? In memory of Ross."

"Er, yeah. I don't see why not. I expect his family will come and get his belongings, but I'm sure they won't mind if you take the plant."

"Thank you."

The front door closed, and Daisy heaved a sigh of relief.

"Well done!" she exclaimed, coming out from her hiding place. "He bought it, thank goodness. I nearly died when you mentioned the potted plant. I thought he might come in here to look at it."

"I knew he wouldn't," said Krish. "He was so uncomfortable, he couldn't wait to get out of the apartment. You should have seen his face when I told him I was Ross's boyfriend."

Daisy smiled. "I can just imagine. Come on, let's get out of here. You hang on to those keys and go out the front. The caretaker will be expecting it. If you see him again, be sure to wave. I'll use the window."

"Are you sure?"

"I don't want to be seen. It'll just complicate matters." And she was sure that nosy old granny would still be peeking out of the upstairs window.

"Okay." He grabbed the potted plant, hugging it to his chest like a teddy bear, only his face visible through the leaves.

"Be careful you don't fall," said Daisy, as she retraced her steps through the living room to the window. She pushed it upwards, and it opened with a creak. Poking her head outside, she made sure no one was around. If it was that snoopy old woman who'd told on them, she might still be lurking in the yard waiting to see what had happened. The two ladies who'd been hanging up their washing had disappeared. A fitted sheet and a pink floral duvet cover hung on the line, flapping in the cold breeze.

Daisy had one leg over the windowsill when her phone buzzed in her pocket. Talk about bad timing. Whoever it was could wait. She ignored it and gingerly squeezed through the gap, lowering herself onto the ground beneath the window. Then she shut the window and glanced around her to check that the coast was still clear. All good. Ducking so she was below the hedge, she made her way around the back of the block toward the garden gate. She let herself out with a soft sigh of relief. They'd made it!

With a spring in her step, she walked back to the car, taking the long way round the block so as not to give that lady another peek at her. Only when she was safely away from the property did she check her phone.

One missed call. DCI McGuinness.

Chapter Twenty

Only once they were at the car, the potted plant stowed away in the trunk, did Daisy return the detective's call.

"Daisy?" He answered straightaway. "I'm going into an interview, so I don't have long."

"Sorry I missed your call," she said, guilt creeping up on her. She ought to tell him what she'd discovered at Ross's apartment, but he was in a hurry and that was an in-depth discussion they needed to have face-to-face. There would be less chance of him getting annoyed that way. "Did you want something?"

"It was just a courtesy call." He spoke fast, his words running together. She could hear talking and typing in the background and gathered he was at the police station.

"Oh?"

"We arrested Yvette Bechard this morning."

"Yvette?" Daisy opened the car door with a beep and slipped inside, but she didn't start the engine. Krish got in beside her. "Why Yvette?"

"I should have thought it was obvious." He sounded impatient. "I said I'll be there in a sec," he yelled to someone in the background. Daisy held the phone away from her ear. "Sorry about that. *You* told us about her relationship with Melanie Haverstock, the bullying and the leaking of information to Betting Direct. You didn't think we were going to ignore that, did you?"

"No, of course not. It's just that, well, I'm not sure Yvette is the murderer. She received a threatening note too."

Krish shook his head like a sheepdog. *No way*, he mouthed.

"She could have sent it to herself to divert suspicion," McGuinness retorted. "Besides, I didn't ask for your opinion, Daisy. I was merely calling to tell you we've made an arrest. I thought you deserved that much." *After what she'd been through*, he meant, but he didn't say it.

"On what grounds was she arrested?" she enquired, drumming her fingers on the steering wheel. They must have something other than Daisy's testimony to have arrested the French boutique owner.

"We searched her clothing store this morning and found Melanie Haverstock's mobile phone. It was locked in a cupboard beneath the cash register."

Daisy stopped drumming. Melanie's phone? At Yvette's boutique?

She stared out of the windscreen at a train speeding past. This case got stranger by the minute. Could it be that she was wrong and Yvette *had* stolen Melanie's phone from the crime scene? But why? Even if she had murdered Melanie, why hold on to her phone? Surely it was damning evidence? Something niggled at the back of her mind, just out of reach.

"That is circumstantial evidence," she finally said. "It doesn't mean Yvette killed her."

What? mouthed Krish.

"No, but she also doesn't have an alibi for the night of the murder, and with your statement, it's enough for an arrest warrant."

Daisy felt bad. If she hadn't mentioned the harassment by Olaf, Yvette might not have been arrested. A train passed in a motion-blur of red and green, causing Daisy to blink and look away.

"Look, I have to go," McGuinness said. "I'll talk to you later."

He hung up before she could tell him about Yvette being at the V&A on Saturday night. He'd get there on his own after Yvette showed him the photographs. She almost felt sorry for the detective, but this was a process he had to go through. At least he was thorough; she couldn't fault him for that.

Daisy glanced at Krish. "The police searched Yvette's boutique and found Melanie's mobile phone. She's been arrested."

Krish gasped. "Oh my gosh." Then he blinked. "What does that mean?"

"I'm not sure. It could be something, but then again, it could be nothing. We know Yvette wasn't involved. She was up in London on Saturday evening—she showed Penny the photographs—and she also received a threatening note."

"There must be a logical explanation," Krish said.

"Yvette would never stab anyone in the back, literally or figuratively. She's far too much of a lady."

She wasn't sure about his rationale, but she knew what he meant. "I agree. McGuinness thinks Yvette took the phone off Melanie at the murder scene, but I just can't see it. Why would she do that?" Then it struck her, and she gasped.

Krish jumped out of the passenger seat. "What?"

"I *knew* there was something odd about that. Melanie had her phone on her when she was killed. It was in her purse, I saw it myself."

Krish's eyes widened. "She had two cell phones?"

Daisy smacked the steering wheel with the flat of her hand. "Yes! Of course, she had two phones. One was for everyday use, while the other was a secret phone to communicate with her lover."

"Mr. Roberts?"

Daisy nodded. It made perfect sense. Mel couldn't risk Douglas finding out about the affair, so she used a second phone that she kept hidden. Daisy was willing to bet that when McGuinness studied the phone records, he'd only find one number that called that phone: the dog-food billionaire himself.

"Why would Yvette take it?"

"That's just it," said Daisy, starting the car. "She wouldn't."

Krish sighed. "I'm not following."

Daisy pulled out of the parking spot. Slowly, things were starting to make sense.

"You know what her phone was doing there, don't you?" said Krish.

"Not completely." Daisy slowed down as they approached a red light. "But I'm getting there. I wish I could speak to Yvette. I want to know if Melanie was at her boutique on Saturday morning, the day of the murder."

"She could have been," said Krish. "Her hair appointment was at ten, so she might have popped next door beforehand. A lot of our customers do, if they're early."

"But I need to be sure." Daisy stepped on the accelerator as the light changed. "McGuinness will know."

"How will he know?"

"Because he's interviewing Yvette as we speak." She didn't envy Yvette being in that dreadful room with McGuinness at his intimidating best across the table from her. "He'll ask her how the victim's phone ended up in her boutique, and Yvette will confirm Melanie was there that morning. I'm betting that's when she lost her phone."

"Lost her phone? Are you saying Melanie left it in the boutique by mistake?"

Daisy nodded.

"Which means Yvette had nothing to do with the murder," finished Krish with a triumphant grin.

"Exactly."

Daisy dropped Krish off at his house on her way to the salon. "Don't lose those keys," she told him sternly. "We are going to need them to back up our story."

It was nearly midday, and poor Asa had been fielding calls and rescheduling appointments all morning. Daisy stopped at Starbucks and bought her assistant a thank-you coffee and grabbed herself a giant blueberry muffin for lunch, before rushing into the salon and greeting a frazzled Asa with an apologetic smile. "Have you been frantic?"

Asa pulled a face. "Yeah, the phone hasn't stopped ringing, and I've had back-to-back nail appointments all morning. Everyone wants Halloween nails. I'm beginning to regret doing this." She flashed her spiderweb fingernails at Daisy.

"Great marketing," Daisy said, handing her a grande coffee with whipped cream and sprinkles. "Here, have a break. You deserve it."

Asa grinned and accepted the drink. "Thanks, boss."

Daisy's first customer arrived at twelve thirty, and because Asa had rescheduled all of Penny and Krish's appointments, the salon was calm and peaceful, creating the perfect atmosphere in which to think. By closing time, Daisy was beginning to piece part of the puzzle together. What she really needed to do was to speak to McGuinness, preferably not at the police station.

She sent him a text message asking if they could meet up, adding that it was important. That way he was less likely to ignore it.

She had just closed the salon and locked the front door when she heard a deep, masculine voice behind her.

"Daisy, I'm glad I caught you."

Niall Barclay stood on the curb looking more Heathcliff than ever in his long dark coat, wild gypsy hair and brooding expression. All that was missing was the howling gale and the backdrop of the moors behind him.

"Oh, hi, Niall," she said with an easy smile. "What are you doing here? Is Penny okay?"

"She's fine." His normally mischievous blue eyes were sombre. "I was wondering if we could talk. Do you want to grab a drink?"

"Sure, it's been a while." They'd attended some of Dame Serena's more raucous parties together in the past, although she had to admit, he'd calmed down since he'd been with Penny, or maybe it was life creeping up on him. He must be almost fifty by now, although he still looked great. His frame was solid, his shoulders broad, and his thighs were strong and muscular from all that horse training. Some men seemed to improve with age.

The corners of his mouth turned up. "That it has."

They strolled together down the high street until they came to a local pub called Ye Olde Ship. It backed onto the River Thames and had a wide balcony where Daisy liked to meet friends for drinks on warm summer evenings. This evening, however, it was already dark, and the temperature had plummeted to a few degrees above freezing. Winter had definitely settled in. They chose a table by the fire. Daisy stood in front of it and rubbed her hands together. She really should buy a new pair of gloves. Yvette's, that's where she'd go. As soon as the boutique owner had been released.

"The horses don't like the cold," Niall told her once he'd gotten them both a drink. "We have to insulate the stables and make sure they have their blankets at night."

A world-class horse breeder, Niall knew horses better than anybody Daisy had ever met. Many of his thoroughbreds had won trophies at prestigious events like Royal Ascot and the Epsom Derby.

"I don't like it either," Daisy complained, turning away from the fire and sitting down. "I can see why my parents moved to the Costa del Sol."

"Maybe you'll follow in their footsteps?" he teased, knowing her relationship with her parents was practically nonexistent. Once, over several bottles of prosecco, she'd told him how they'd up and left as soon as she'd finished school to live on a golf estate in sunny Malaga. They'd never had much of an input anyway, and she didn't miss them. It was one of the things she and Floria had in common. Absent parents. "How's your golf swing coming on?"

She shook her head. "Nope, my life is here. I have no intention of giving everything up and emigrating to Spain. And for your information, I can't play golf."

He chuckled. "It's good to see you, Daisy."

"So, what did you want to talk about?" she asked, after taking a long, satisfying sip of chenin blanc.

He hesitated, then said, "I'm worried about Penny. Until this is resolved, I don't think she should be alone. This attacker could have killed her, and there's no saying he won't try again."

"I couldn't agree more," Daisy said.

He studied her across the table. "What is going on, Daisy? Rumours are flying around like wildfire. First Penny was a suspect, then you were arrested, now Yvette Bechard is in custody. Does McGuinness know what he's doing?"

It did seem a bit ridiculous. "It's complicated," she said. "They searched Yvette's boutique and found Melanie Haverstock's cell phone. Melanie was the one who told Betting Direct that the boutique was going under."

"So, Yvette killed Melanie in revenge for ruining her business?"

"I don't believe Yvette is the murderer, Niall," she said, taking another sip of her wine. The fire was making her feel warm and toasty. "McGuinness has got the wrong person."

"Again?" He threw her an exasperated glance.

"I'm afraid so."

"Who is the murderer, then?" he asked. "Do you have any idea?"

She sighed. "No, but I do know it wasn't Yvette or Penny or me."

"He'll run out of suspects soon," he scoffed, taking a swig of his lager.

"Exactly. There are only so many people it can be," she said. "It's a process of elimination. I'm sure DCI McGuinness will get there in the end."

He rolled his eyes. "I like the man, but he really got my back up asking me if I'd cancelled on Pen last Saturday night. Why would Penny lie? She's the most honest person I know. I was up to my elbows in horse placenta, for goodness' sake."

Daisy laughed. "Congratulations. Penny told me about the baby foal."

He grinned, and for the first time all evening it actually reached his eyes. "Yeah, she's going to be a prize winner like her mummy."

He would know.

"Anyway," Niall continued, "I've asked Pen to come and stay with me for a while, just until this investigation is over and the culprit is behind bars."

"Good idea," said Daisy. At least that way Penny would be surrounded by Niall's staff, grooms, riders, and a stack of other people. The killer would have a hard time getting to her there.

"Except she's said no."

"Oh dear. Why?"

"Apparently, it's too soon. She doesn't want to impose on me. You know what she's like." His eyes searched hers, looking for confirmation.

Daisy did, but Penny was smart too. Niall's history with women was sketchy, at best. He grew bored quickly and moved on faster than one of his prized stallions racing for the finish line. Penny was playing it cool, taking it slow, keeping Niall interested. But in this case, she thought Penny staying at Niall's place was worth the risk. There was a killer out there, and Penny had been attacked before.

"I'll talk to her," she said.

"Thanks, Daisy." He sighed in relief. "I feel so helpless. It would give me massive peace of mind if she were to come and stay at Gresham. She's being discharged tomorrow morning."

Gresham Stables was his estate on the other side of Esher, near Cobham. It was comprised of acres of farmland, complete with a renovated farmhouse that was more like a mansion, tennis courts, and of course, state-of-the-art stables and training facilities. She'd been to a few parties there with Floria in the past, usually very classy events with the well-heeled horse-racing set.

They finished their drinks and said goodbye. Daisy was walking across the frosty meadow when her phone buzzed. It was McGuinness.

I'll be at yours at nine. Can't make it any earlier.

She replied: *See you then.*

Chapter Twenty-one

"What is so urgent, Daisy?" McGuinness asked, striding into her living room in his black coat glittering with moisture. It had begun to rain shortly after she'd arrived home, and the storm was now whipping against the windows in a constant torrent.

"I need to talk to you about Yvette Bechard and Ross Monroe," she said, getting straight to the point. McGuinness had driven from Guildford after a long, hard day to get there. He looked weary, the now-familiar dark rings beneath his eyes making them appear even more stormy, and his five o'clock shadow long past the acceptable length.

He blinked, Ross's name throwing him a bit. "What has Ross got to do with Yvette?" he asked.

"I'll explain." She took his coat and hung it on the

hook. "First, can I get you a cup of tea? No offense, but you look like you need one."

"That would be great." He ran a hand through his hair, sending droplets flying onto the rug. "It's been a hell of a day."

Daisy made them each a cup and laid out a dish of biscuits as well, figuring the detective would be hungry after a long day at the precinct. She was right. He fell on them like a ravenous hyena.

"Don't they feed you at the police station?" she joked.

He gave a wry smile. "I haven't had time to eat today. It's been one thing after the next."

"Is Yvette still in custody?" she asked him.

He grimaced. "No, we had to let her go. There was nothing to hold her on. I don't mind telling you, I'm getting a hell of a lot of flak from my superiors about this. I have to make an arrest soon—and preferably the right one this time."

"Did she show you the photographs of the V&A exhibition?"

He gave her a sideways glance. "You knew about her alibi?"

"She showed Penny the pictures yesterday afternoon. I take it they were time-stamped?"

He scoffed. "Thanks for the heads-up."

"I tried to tell you, but you were in such a hurry I couldn't get a word in edgeways. Besides, knowing you, you'd still have hauled her in for questioning."

He didn't reply.

Daisy watched while he sipped his tea and had another biscuit. It couldn't be easy having to answer to the powers that be at the same time as trying to concentrate on the case. She knew the pressure the police were under at the moment, particularly with the surge in knife crime around the country. Statistics mattered. Arrests mattered. At least she didn't have that problem.

"Can I ask you a question?" she began.

"If this is about the investigation, you know I can't answer it."

"Off the record, then," she said. "Was Melanie at Yvette's boutique earlier on Saturday morning?"

He stared at her. "How on earth did you know that?"

She couldn't resist a smile. "The mobile phone. I knew Yvette wasn't the killer, and the only other explanation was that Melanie had visited the salon earlier that day and lost her phone while she was there."

"I should have thought of that," he admitted with a tired shake of his head. "It's logical when you think about it. I jumped to the conclusion that she must have taken it from the victim at the crime scene." His shoulders sagged. "It was wishful thinking on my part."

His expression was so glum, Daisy had to resist the urge to give him a hug. She softened her voice. "Except Melanie had a phone in her handbag, remember? We saw it at the crime scene when you looked inside her purse?"

McGuinness nodded. "I remembered that, but I figured she must have had two. One for the lover."

"Yes, I thought that too," Daisy said. "It makes sense."

There was a pause, during which the only sound was McGuinness crunching his biscuit.

"Can I share a theory with you?" Daisy watched as he swallowed and reached for his tea. He glanced up, sighed, then put his cup back down. "Why not? I'm all out of ideas right now. This investigation is going around in circles."

It wasn't like Paul to be so despondent. The pressure

to find the culprit was obviously weighing heavily on him, and so far, he'd wrongly arrested two suspects and questioned a third.

"Okay. Well, I was thinking about what might have happened that night outside my salon. In particular, why Melanie was there—and I think I know."

His eyes widened. "Go on."

"Imagine this. Melanie arrives at her hair appointment on Saturday morning, but she's early. She has a few minutes to spare, so she pops into Yvette's boutique to have a look around. While she's there, she loses her phone. Maybe it fell out of her handbag or pocket, or perhaps she put it down to look at something. Who knows?"

McGuinness didn't take his eyes off her.

"Then, she comes to her hair appointment, which was two hours long 'cause she had a complicated colour job. At midday, she leaves for her illicit rendezvous with Roy Roberts, Liz's husband. It's Saturday afternoon, and Roy has been at the rugby club all morning, but he leaves and meets her at a pre-agreed-upon location, probably a hotel. They . . ." She smiled. "Well, you get the picture."

He grunted.

"Afterwards, Melanie realises she's lost her second phone, the one she uses to contact Roy. It's not in the hotel room, so she thinks back to where she might have left it."

"The salon," McGuinness finished for her.

Daisy clicked her fingers. "Exactly. So, she comes back to the salon to see if I'm still there. At this point, it's probably around eight forty-five. Any earlier and I would have seen her. Penny was there until eight, and I was busy with Liz, who left shortly after eight thirty. I'm clearing up, probably in the back, so I don't hear her. She can't get in the front door because it's already locked. So, what does she do?"

"She goes around to the back." McGuinness's eyes had recovered some of their sparkle.

"Exactly. And that's when the killer strikes," Daisy finished, reaching for a biscuit and popping it into her mouth.

"Very good." McGuinness gave her an admiring look. "I'm almost too scared to ask, but do you have any idea who the killer is?"

"No, not yet," mumbled Daisy, her mouth full of biscuit.

"Not yet?"

She shrugged. "I'm working on it."

McGuinness rubbed his forehead. "What is it you're not telling me, Daisy?"

"What makes you think I'm not telling you something?"

"I know you, and I've warned you before about withholding evidence."

She hesitated. He was going to go ballistic when he found out how they'd snooped around Ross's apartment, but she had to tell him. There was no other way. Taking a deep breath, she said, "Okay, but promise you won't get upset."

He frowned. "Now I'm really worried."

"It's nothing illegal," she rushed out, hoping he didn't notice how her voice had ticked up a notch. His look said he didn't believe her. She took a deep breath. *Here goes . . .*

"Krish and I didn't believe Ross's death was an isolated event," she began. "I'm sorry, Paul, but it's too much of a coincidence that it happened the same night as the attack on Penny."

He sighed. "I didn't have the evidence I needed to take over the case. Surbiton wanted it, and for me to assume control, I had to prove it was linked to Melanie Haverstock's death, which I couldn't do. My hands were tied."

"But mine weren't."

His gaze darkened. "What did you do?"

She mentally crossed her fingers. "Ross had given Krish a key to his apartment, so we went round to see if we could find anything that might link him to Melanie or her killer."

McGuinness leaned forward and said slowly, "Krish had a key to Ross's apartment?"

"Yes, they were . . . in a relationship."

"Ah." He sat back but didn't lose the suspicious glare. "And what did you discover?"

"You won't believe this." She picked up her mobile phone and showed him the photograph she'd taken of his desk drawer.

He sucked in his breath. "Is this for real?"

She nodded. "Ross was the one writing the 'murderer' notes. This is the exact same notepaper and pens."

"But why?" He scratched his head.

Daisy sympathised. When she'd first seen the offending stationery, she'd also struggled to make sense of it.

"Ross had nothing to do with Melanie or the investigation. How did he even know who the suspects were?"

"Guess?" Daisy raised an eyebrow.

"Krish." He sighed. "I should have known."

"Not that it's any consolation, but I think he's learned his lesson," she added. "He was pretty cut up by Ross's death. There are limits to pillow talk."

"Did you touch these?" McGuinness asked, nodding to the photo on Daisy's phone.

"Of course not," she lied. It would not be a good idea to mention the latex gloves at this point. They'd blow her story right out the window.

"Good. I'll get on the phone to Surbiton and send Forensics over there ASAP. They'll have no choice but to hand over the case now. Great work, Daisy." He pulled out his phone and stood up. "Excuse me while I make a few calls."

She left him to it and went into the kitchen, where she set about preparing cheese and pickle sandwiches, which she put on a plate with some potato crisps. McGuinness must be starving, not having eaten all day, and those few biscuits wouldn't have filled him up. Placing the plate on the counter, she made them both another cup of tea, then perched on one of the bar stools to wait.

He gave her a thumbs-up and took a sandwich, the phone still glued to his ear. He munched between sentences, pacing up and down the living room as he spoke. From what she could gather, Surbiton had agreed to hand over the stabbing.

Hanging up, he grinned, "Got it. Now we can get SOCO out."

The scene of crime officers agreed to go around to the apartment first thing in the morning to collect evidence. It was still pelting down outside, and this wasn't a live crime scene, so it didn't warrant immediate action.

"I would have preferred today, but tomorrow is soon enough," McGuinness said as he re-pocketed his phone and reached for another sandwich. "You're a star, Daisy. I needed this." He grinned and heaved himself up onto the other bar stool.

"My pleasure." His mood had improved considerably, thanks to the new development and the sustenance. It was nice to see him smile again.

"The big question is, why?" McGuinness said, his mouth full.

"I've been thinking," Daisy mused, her hands wrapped around her teacup. "And I have a theory about that too."

He laughed. "Of course you do."

She supressed a grin. "Do you want to hear it or not?"

"Please, go ahead." He took the last sandwich and bit into it.

"What if Ross was blackmailing the suspects?"

McGuinness stopped chewing.

"Think about it," she said slowly. "Why else would he want to know everything about the investigation? What if he sent all the possible suspects a 'murderer' note and finally hit on the right person to blackmail?"

"The killer?" McGuinness said.

"And that person tracked him down and stabbed him," Daisy finished.

There was a pause as McGuinness thought about this for a moment. Eventually, he said, "You might be on to something. Once he got the names from Krish, it would have been easy enough to look up people's addresses."

"Especially since he's in banking. He'd have access to lots of financial information. I'm sure Krish innocently helped him out too." She jumped off the bar stool. "And I saw him in the high street the day Yvette received her note! Yes, that's right. He was coming out of the Party Palace with Krish. It was around lunchtime, and shortly after that, I went into Yvette's and found her sobbing on the floor."

"It ties in with your theory," mused McGuinness.

"Now we just have to find out who else he blackmailed, other than you, Liz Roberts, and Yvette."

"We're running out of suspects," Daisy said, climbing back onto her bar stool.

"Let's work by process of elimination." McGuinness rested his forearms on the countertop. "Starting with you."

"I was the most obvious suspect," Daisy said, wrapping her hands around her cup. "Which is why I got the first note, but I called you immediately afterwards."

"Which ruled you out because the real killer wouldn't call the police."

She gasped. "I bet that was Ross hiding in the bushes that night, waiting to gauge my reaction."

"Makes sense."

"Next was Liz, and she came to see me," Daisy continued. "So, Ross knew it wasn't her either. The real murderer would keep the note to themselves. They wouldn't run to tell a friend."

McGuinness nodded in agreement.

Daisy continued, "Poor Yvette collapsed in floods of tears when she discovered the note, and once again, Ross was around to see it."

"Sly bastard."

"And Penny was attacked, so Ross would have known she wasn't the culprit." Daisy glanced across at McGuinness. "Whom does that leave?"

"Only the three girls from the bachelorette party and your friend Donna, whom we can discount because she was giving a performance on Saturday night."

"Krish would have told Ross that it couldn't have been her," said Daisy. "Besides, Donna would have told me if she'd received a note."

"Which leaves the three models," finished McGuinness.

They gazed at each other as the reality sank in. It had to be one of them; they were the only suspects left on the list.

"We need to check to see if they received notes too." McGuinness's voice was low.

"I think we can assume all three did," said Daisy quietly. "And one retaliated."

McGuinness looked grim. "The killer?"

"I think it's very likely," she said. "Don't you?"

McGuinness scratched his chin. "I interviewed all three of them on Monday, and nobody knew Melanie Haverstock. There is no connection between any of them and the victim. I don't understand it. Are we quite sure?"

"There isn't anyone else." Daisy racked her brains, mentally ticking everyone who came into the salon off her list. "Clayton was at home all evening. Krish would have told Ross that, I'm sure, which is why Clayton didn't get a note. Penny's last client was Zoe, but again, she was never a suspect because she went out for dinner with her husband that night."

"I checked with the restaurant. Zoe and her husband arrived at eight and left at ten," McGuinness confirmed, sweeping imaginary crumbs off the countertop. "I couldn't get any sense out of Clayton's mother, the old lady is too far gone to provide much of an alibi, but I agree, she couldn't have been left alone. And the carer confirmed she left at six, when Clayton got home. The only three I didn't check out properly were the girls, because none of them knew the victim."

"One of them is lying," stated Daisy.

McGuinness's brow crinkled in concentration. "There's

got to be a connection between one of them and the victim, a motive we haven't found yet."

There was a small pause as Daisy contemplated his words. If there was a motive, she didn't know what it was. Then a thought occurred to her. "I don't think you should ask them if they received a note. It might tip off the murderer that we're on to them."

"Hmm . . ." McGuinness turned toward her. "I could arrest all three and bring them in for questioning."

Daisy chuckled. "I know you like arresting people, but what would your boss think of that?"

"True, I have been charging people left, right, and centre lately. It would be better to hit on the right culprit this time, if at all possible."

She held up a finger. "I have an idea."

He raised his eyebrows. "What do you suggest?"

"Fancy a trip to Esher?"

Chapter Twenty-two

Daisy sat beside McGuinness as he drove his no-nonsense BMW to Esher in the pouring rain. The windscreen wipers whipped back and forth, but they were barely fast enough to clear the screen before it was drenched again. He put the blue grate lights on, more to warn other motorists that they were coming than because it was an emergency. The roads were dark, and traffic was scarce. Most people had decided to stay indoors out of the late autumn squall.

"You're sure they are working tonight?" McGuinness asked. Daisy had told him about the barmen Mickey and Stu, both of whom had been on duty the night of the hen-do.

Daisy nodded. "Yes, they both work every night except Sundays and Mondays. I checked their rota last time I was here."

"And you're convinced one of them is lying?"

"They must be. If Apple, Ferne, or Paloma killed Melanie, they can't all have been in the pub that night. One of them must have left to go back to Edgemead. It's the only possible explanation."

"Agatha Christie said something about the 'only possible outcome' in one of her books, didn't she?" McGuinness mused as the dark and rain-drenched Hinchley Wood flashed by. "I can't remember exactly what it was now."

"She said that the impossible could not have happened, therefore the impossible must be possible in spite of appearances."

"That's it." He chuckled.

When they got closer to the pub, Daisy shifted uneasily in her chair. "The day of Paloma's wedding, I mentioned Melanie to the three girls, and none of them blinked an eye. They had no idea who she was. I'm usually a good judge of people, so it's crazy to think that one of them was lying."

"You *are* a good judge of people," he said. "Unfortunately, some people are just incredibly good liars." His voice hardened. "Let's see what the barmen have to say once we apply a little pressure."

Daisy nodded. It seemed the wool had been pulled over her eyes too.

McGuinness parked the car in front of the pub, and they got out. Daisy took a deep breath of cold air and felt it go right down into her lungs. Things were about to get interesting.

"Let's start with Stu," suggested Daisy, once they were inside. It was hot and crowded, and they had to fight their way through throngs of overexcited people to the bar. It was ten thirty, and the pub was in full swing.

Daisy spotted Mickey immediately. He had his hands full processing a big order of drinks. Stu was farther down the bar at the other end, pouring a pint of lager.

McGuinness asked to speak to the manager, and five minutes later, a nervous Stu was following them to a backroom office. Daisy shivered as they walked in. It was cold compared to the heat and activity in the bar, but McGuinness didn't seem to mind. It would only make the witness more uncomfortable. She'd read a lot about interrogation tactics in her course and had picked up a thing or two from her own recent experiences. It would be a long time before she forgot that freezing interview room and the metal chair.

"Explain to me what you can remember about the three ladies who were here last Saturday night," began McGuinness, sitting at the manager's desk. He read out their names.

Stu shivered in a T-shirt opposite him, while Daisy stood by the door and observed.

"I came on at five," he said, folding his arms across his chest. "The girls arrived around seven, but I can't be sure of the exact time."

"What state were they in?" questioned McGuinness. Daisy had filled him in on her previous discussion with Stu, so he knew the gist of it.

"They were drunk already. Apple was worse than the others, but we served them anyway, or rather Mickey did. I saw him give them a bottle of champagne. I didn't think they needed any more, but . . ." He shrugged. "It's not my place to tell them what to do. It was a hen-do, after all, and you know how raucous those can be."

"Quite," said McGuinness. "What happened next?"

He hesitated, then glanced at Daisy. "I didn't tell you this before, because I didn't want to get Mickey into trouble."

Daisy stared at him. "What didn't you tell me?"

"Well, Mickey disappeared for half an hour or so between eight and nine. I can't be sure exactly when, but I know it was after my smoke break at eight because he asked me to cover for him. He was making out with some girl in the wine cellar."

"You're absolutely certain he was in the cellar?" asked McGuinness, frowning. "He hadn't left the pub?"

"Yes, quite sure. When he wasn't back by nine, I thumped on the door. He came out with lipstick all over his face, and there was a woman hiding behind the crates of wine. I heard her giggling."

"Did you see her?" they both asked at the same time. Daisy approached the desk and perched on the corner.

"No, he didn't open the door wide enough for me to get a good look. I just assumed it was one of the regulars. He flirts with all the local girls. They love him." He gave a rather rueful smile.

McGuinness paused for a moment, then said, "I want you to think very carefully about this next question, Stu. Did you serve the girls during this time?"

He shook his head. "No, I was worked off my feet. The bar was heaving. I don't know where the girls got to. I assumed they were at a table somewhere."

"But they weren't at the bar?" cut in Daisy.

He shook his head. "I don't think so."

Daisy met McGuinness's eye.

"Penny said you helped her to the ladies' room with

Apple later that night. Can you remember what time?" the detective asked.

"Yeah, that was after Penny got here, so about nine thirty. Apple was puking her guts out, poor thing. Those models don't eat enough to handle their booze."

That was probably true.

"So, all three girls were accounted for at that point," McGuinness said to no one in particular.

Stu answered anyway. "Yeah, Ferne and Paloma were at the bar with Mickey. I remember, because when I got back, he was seeing off a bloke who was hitting on Paloma."

"The bride?" asked McGuinness.

He nodded. "Mickey was really angry. He called a bouncer to have the guy removed."

"Was he aggressive? The bloke, I mean?"

"No, just drunk and horny. He meant no harm. The bouncer escorted him out, and that was the end of it."

"What about Ferne? Was she there too?" Daisy asked.

"Yes, they both were."

McGuinness drummed his fingers on the desk, deep in thought. A long moment passed, then Stu shifted awkwardly in his chair. "Is that it? Can I go?"

McGuinness nodded. "Yeah, you can go. Send in Mickey."

Stu left, throwing Daisy a sheepish grin.

"If Mickey was fooling around with a girl in the wine cellar and Stu was busy serving customers, any one of the girls could have left the bar," said Daisy. "The problem is, we don't know which one."

"We're going to have to question the girls," said McGuinness.

"'We?'" Daisy smiled.

He cleared his throat. "I mean I'm going to have to question the girls."

There was a knock on the door, and Mickey stalked in. His head was held at an arrogant angle, and Daisy knew he had gone into defence mode. McGuinness must have known it, too, because he didn't waste any time in breaking him down.

"Sit down," he barked, making Daisy jump. She slid off the corner of the desk and stood behind McGuinness with her back to the wall.

Mickey looked uncertainly at Daisy, then took a seat. "Look, mate, I don't know what this is about, but . . ."

"I'm not your mate," McGuinness snapped, fixing his steely glare on Mickey. "You can call me 'DCI McGuinness' or 'sir.'"

"Sorry, sir," Mickey corrected. Daisy masked a smile. It wouldn't hurt to have Mickey pulled down a few notches.

"This is a murder enquiry," the detective said. "So, I suggest you tell us the truth or risk being arrested for perverting the course of justice. Is that clear?" His gaze didn't waver. Damn, he was good.

Mickey swallowed, then nodded. There was no trace of arrogance now.

"Who was with you in the wine cellar on Saturday night?"

Mickey bit his lip but didn't reply.

McGuinness waited. Eventually, Mickey mumbled, "I can't say, sir."

McGuinness slammed his hand down on the desk, making Mickey jump. Daisy's pulse accelerated.

"Do you want to continue this conversation at the police station?" He took a pair of handcuffs out of his jacket pocket and laid them on the desk.

"No, I don't. It's just . . . It would be compromising her to say," he stammered.

"You will be compromising a lot more if you don't answer," McGuinness replied.

"It's really important, Mickey," Daisy said, pushing herself away from the wall and walking around the desk.

Mickey looked beseechingly up at her. "I really want to help, Daisy, but . . ." He shook his head.

"It's not worth getting arrested over." Daisy rested her hand on his shoulder. "Trust me, I've been there."

He seemed to weigh this up for a moment, then sighed and began to talk. When he was done, Daisy met McGuinness's gaze over Mickey's head.

The impossible had suddenly become possible.

Chapter Twenty-three

Daisy invited Apple, Ferne, and Paloma to the hair salon the next day under the pretence of a free wash and blow-dry. McGuinness could have had them all arrested and taken in for questioning, but Daisy thought the nonconfrontational approach was better. Besides, they still didn't have a motive, even though they now knew who the perpetrator was. Daisy hoped the surprise discussion would catch the killer off guard and she would reveal why she'd killed Melanie Haverstock.

Niall brought Penny, who was out of the hospital and looking much better. She was under strict orders not to do anything strenuous for the next few weeks to give her concussion time to heal, but other than that, she was back to her normal self.

Krish, Asa, and Bianca were all present, along with a

grey-faced Douglas Haverstock, who'd been dropped off by his sister. Liz Roberts sat at the back, trying not to draw attention to herself, but her darting eyes belied how curious she was to know who'd killed the woman who had been sleeping with her husband. Since she'd received a threatening note and had also been quizzed by the police, Daisy thought she deserved to be in at the conclusion.

Yvette was there too, impeccably made up as usual and showing no sign of her recent ordeal at the Guildford Police Station. Next to her sat Floria, brightening up the room in a fuchsia coat, her blond hair in pretty curls around her face. For once, she wasn't talking, her blue eyes flitting from person to person with abject curiosity.

Also present was DCI McGuinness, who looked formidable and just a bit dashing in a dark suit and tie, along with Sergeant Buckley, who couldn't stop fidgeting and was eyeing out the industrial hair dryer like it was an alien spaceship.

"What is this?" asked Ferne when she walked into the salon and saw the gathering.

"Take a seat." Daisy gestured to one of the vacant swivel chairs her customers sat in when they had their hair done. Ferne looked like she might refuse, but then pulled a sour face and sat down.

Apple arrived next and skidded to a halt inside the entrance. "Are we having a party?" she asked Daisy.

"Not today, Apple," said Daisy. "Please sit down."

Paloma was the last to arrive. She waltzed through the door, a pink pashmina wrapped around her neck, her glossy dark hair up in a high ponytail. No one could miss the enormous diamond on her ring finger, accompanied by a glittering wedding band. "Oh, hello," she said, glancing around at the little crowd. "Did I miss something?"

"No, you're in good time." McGuinness stood up. "Now that everybody is here, I thought I'd introduce myself. For those of you who don't know me, I'm Detective Chief Inspector McGuinness from the Guildford Police Station."

There was a tense silence. Paloma glanced at Penny, confused. Penny didn't meet her eye. Instead, she gripped Niall's hand and bit her lip. Asa looked terrified, while Krish stared transfixed at McGuinness. Bianca, who wouldn't have been there had she not been working today, filed her nails.

"Thanks for coming." He glanced around the group. "I got Daisy to ask you here today so we could discuss the events of last Saturday evening."

"What happened last Saturday?" asked Apple.

"You mean the hen night?" Paloma enquired.

"Why are we discussing that?" Ferne asked.

McGuinness ignored the barrage of questions. "You all came here to have your hair done that morning, is that correct?"

All three nodded, reminding Daisy of those teeny toy dogs with the bobbing heads.

"And one of you stole a pair of hair-cutting scissors belonging to Daisy." He fixed his silver gaze on them, one by one.

"What?" blurted out Paloma. "That's ridiculous. Why would we do that?"

"To murder Melanie Haverstock," the detective said softly.

The three girls stared at him blankly. Finally, Apple asked, "Is she your friend who passed away, Daisy?"

Daisy smiled at her. "Yes, that's right. You have a good memory."

"What's that got to do with us?" asked Ferne.

"Quite a bit, actually," McGuinness replied. "As you'll find out, if you let me continue."

They lapsed into silence. Daisy had to give it to him, he certainly knew how to intimidate a suspect. In the world of hardened criminals, that was a handy trait to have. In dealing with the general public, not so much, but she was beginning to understand him a little better.

"Melanie Haverstock was found stabbed to death with Daisy's scissors a little after nine on Saturday evening in the back alley."

There was a collective gasp from the girls.

"What? Here?" Paloma's eyes were huge.

Douglas paled, and Liz's eyes narrowed.

"You didn't say she was murdered," Apple cried, looking at Daisy.

McGuinness held up a hand.

"Sorry," she mumbled, and fiddled with the pendant around her neck.

"She'd come back to look for her cell phone, which she'd lost earlier in the day. Of course, she'd left it at Yvette's boutique next door, but she didn't know that. She thought she'd left it at the salon. Daisy had already locked up, so Melanie tried to get Daisy's attention via the back door."

"Except I didn't hear her on account of the rain," Daisy added.

"That's right. Now, this is where it gets interesting," McGuinness continued, all eyes on him. "The killer arrives, sees Melanie in the alleyway, and stabs her in the back."

Douglas closed his eyes. He still had that pale, haunted look of a man consumed by grief. Poor guy. It must be very hard on him to have to relive his wife's murder in front of all these people. She hoped he wasn't going to start bawling again.

McGuinness said, "She falls to the ground, only to be discovered by Daisy after she locks up, a short time later."

Daisy nodded. Nobody spoke. McGuinness let the silence draw out, then he said, "Now, let's go back a couple of hours to the Bear in Esher, where Apple, Ferne, Penny, and Paloma celebrated the bride-to-be's bachelorette party."

All three girls stared at him with a mixture of confusion and wariness.

"You were very drunk, Apple," he said, not unkindly, to the petite blonde, who dropped her head and refused to look at anyone.

"Can't handle my drink," she mumbled. "Never have been able to."

"Consequently, you were in no state to kill anyone. In fact, you spent the better part of the evening throwing up in the ladies' toilet, is that right?"

She nodded miserably. "Penny stayed with me."

"That's right," he acknowledged, giving Penny a curt nod. "Paloma, what were you doing between eight and nine that night?"

"I was drinking tequila shots at the bar with Mickey, the barman, and Ferne," she said, tossing her ponytail over her shoulder.

"Were you?"

Paloma felt the full power of McGuinness's stare and

fidgeted, loosening the pashmina around her neck. "Yes, I was. Ferne can vouch for me."

Ferne nodded. "Yeah, we were getting plastered at the bar. It's all a bit of a blur, to be honest, but Mickey was there. In fact, he kicked some drunk bloke out who was hitting on Paloma."

McGuinness didn't miss a beat. "That was after nine, because Penny was in the ladies' room with Apple by that stage. What were you doing *before* nine o'clock, Paloma?"

Everybody in the room stared at her. She flushed, and said, "I told you, I was at the bar. Why do you keep asking me that?"

"Because you're lying, Paloma," Daisy said quietly. "You were in the wine cellar with Mickey, weren't you?"

She gasped. "No! Of course not. It was my hen night, remember?"

"Are you mad?" Ferne spoke up. "She was right beside me all night. I'd have known if she'd gone off with the barman."

"It's admirable wanting to defend your friend," said McGuinness, "but it's too late for that. Mickey told us everything."

"Oh, the idiot," Paloma fumed, her beautiful face going bright red. "I'll kill him for this."

"Bad choice of words," drawled Niall, who up until this point had remained silent. Floria snorted.

"Please don't tell my husband," she begged. "It was last-minute wedding nerves. I was freaking out, and Mickey helped calm me down, then one thing led to another . . . I swear it was a once-off, a mistake."

"That's why Mickey was so upset with the drunk man who hit on you," said Daisy. "He was jealous."

She nodded sullenly.

"So, if you were in the restroom with Mickey between eight and nine on Saturday night, that leaves you without an alibi, Ferne?" McGuinness shifted his gaze to the slender brunette. "By covering for Paloma, you were actually giving yourself an alibi."

Ferne stared at him. "Rubbish, I was at the bar. Ask Stu, he was there with me."

"With Mickey out of the picture, Stu was too busy tending to the other customers to know where you were," McGuinness told her. "You had plenty of time to drive back to Edgemead and kill Melanie."

Another gasp, this time from the whole room.

"*You* killed Melanie?" shouted Douglas, getting up from his chair. His face was twisted into a desolate grimace. "Why? What did she ever do to you?"

"Nothing. I don't even know Melanie," Ferne retaliated. "This is crazy. I swear I was at the bar. It was pouring with rain, why on earth would I drive all the way back to Edgemead to kill a woman I've never even met?"

"She's got a point." Niall turned to McGuinness. "Are you sure you've got the right woman this time?"

The detective threw him a withering glare. "Yes, quite sure." Then he turned back to Ferne. "I honestly don't know why you did it, Ferne, all I know is that you did. And I can prove it."

"No, you can't." Ferne stood up to face him, her eyes blazing. "Because it's not true. I arrived at the pub in a cab with Paloma and Apple. I didn't even have my car."

"It's true," piped up Apple. "We went together."

"You might not be aware of this," said McGuinness, "but the police have recently installed ANPR cameras on the road between Esher and Edgemead."

"Good heavens, really?" said Niall.

Liz cleared her throat. "That would be my doing. The traffic situation was out of control."

"What is that?" blurted out Asa, her eyes wide. "Is it like CCTV?"

"Kind of," said McGuinness. "They photograph every vehicle's number plate as it drives past, which allows the police to monitor the traffic and track stolen vehicles or vehicles used in crimes."

Ferne was silent.

McGuinness got to his feet. Even though Ferne was tall, he had a good few inches on her. "Your number plate showed up on that road at eight thirty-two on Saturday night."

Apple cried out. "Ferne?"

Paloma stared at Ferne, her mouth open.

"You may have arrived at the bar by cab, but you left in your own vehicle. You must have parked it there during the day. When Paloma was busy with Mickey, and Apple was being sick in the ladies', you drove to Daisy's hair salon and murdered Melanie Haverstock with the scissors you'd stolen earlier that morning."

Ferne shook her head. "No. It's not true."

"It was your car, Ferne," Daisy whispered. "There's no doubt about it."

"But why?" cried Douglas again. "Why my Melanie?"

Still, Ferne didn't speak.

"Because it wasn't Melanie you wanted to kill, was it, Ferne?" Daisy's soft voice penetrated the silence.

McGuinness jerked his head towards her. "What?"

Floria gasped.

"Oh, my giddy aunt," muttered Krish, reaching for Asa's hand.

Ferne shuffled from one foot to the other. Daisy continued, "You thought it was Penny. You were coming to kill her, weren't you?"

Penny gasped. Niall sat bolt upright in his chair. Liz's mouth fell open.

"What are you talking about, Daisy?" asked McGuinness.

She turned to him. He deserved an explanation. "We knew Ferne was the killer, but we didn't know why. There didn't seem to be any motive for killing Melanie, and that's because there wasn't one. She never intended to kill Melanie, that was never the plan."

"Ferne?" Penny whispered, her face deathly pale in the bright lighting of the salon.

"Of course, the hair," blurted out Krish.

Daisy nodded at him. "Exactly. Earlier that morning, Melanie had a radical makeover. She changed her dyed-blond hair to a deep, rich-toned red, which suited her colouring so much better."

"She did look amazing," agreed Krish. Asa nodded.

"The only problem was, it looked a lot like Penny's hair, especially in the dark and wet from the rain."

McGuinness groaned.

"So, when Ferne snuck down the alleyway, she thought it was Penny leaving the salon. Penny was due to work until nine last Saturday night, but I let her go early on account of the hen party."

"That's right," said Penny. "I left early to go home and change because I was meeting you later." She glanced at Niall, who squeezed her leg.

"Except as we know, that didn't happen." Daisy glanced at Niall, who nodded.

"Crashing Thunder went into labour," he said.

"Who's that?" asked Buckley.

"She's my prize mare."

Buckley blinked and turned back to his boss, who gave a little shake of his head, as if to say, *don't ask*.

"You bitch," spat Ferne suddenly, darting towards Penny. She came to a halt a metre in front of her. "You have everything so easy, don't you? You have no idea what it's like to struggle."

"What do you mean?" Penny said, standing up. Niall jumped to his feet beside her.

Ferne's face was an unattractive shade of fuchsia. "Agents are falling over themselves to sign you, everybody wants you in their campaigns, and most of the time you turn the jobs down!" There was incredulity in her voice. "You don't even want to be a model. How is that fair?"

Penny stared at her, but Ferne wasn't done yet. "I starve myself to an inch of my life to get anyone's attention, and then I'm usually the second choice, the backup girl they call when the real model cancels at the last minute." She was inches away from Penny now, shouting in her face. "How do you think that makes me feel?"

Penny reached out to her, but Niall put a warning hand on her arm.

Ferne didn't even notice, she was so consumed with rage. All the pent-up anger, hurt, and aggression she'd suppressed over the years came pouring out. "I live in a crappy council flat, while you spend your time in your luxury apartment or swanning around with him, a man who should have been mine!"

"What?" blurted out Niall.

Ferne turned towards him, her voice softening just a little bit. "I found you first. We hooked up after the *Horse and Hound* shoot, remember?"

"That was a fling," said Niall. "You knew it was nothing serious."

"For you, maybe," she spat. "I wanted more. Much more. Except then you met *her*, and everything changed. You forgot all about me." Tears sprang into her eyes. If it wasn't for the crazy expression on her face, Daisy would have felt sorry for her.

"I had no idea how you felt," whispered Penny.

"No, well, you wouldn't, would you? All you think about is yourself."

"That's not fair," snapped Niall, his body fraught with tension. "You knew exactly where we stood. I'm sorry you got hurt, but we were over long before I got together with Penny." He took Penny's hand, which only served to throw Ferne into an even greater rage.

"You get everything you want, don't you?" she spat, turning on the redhead. "You've never had to work a day in your life. Not really. And this place? This is a hobby for you. You make enough modelling so that you can afford to fanny around here pretending to be a hairdresser, but it's all make-believe."

"That's enough," barked Niall, taking a step forward to put himself between the crazy-eyed Ferne and his girlfriend. Daisy glanced at McGuinness. How long was he going to let this charade continue? If he didn't step in, someone was going to get hurt, and she didn't think it was going to be Penny. Niall was about to explode.

McGuinness came to his senses and grabbed Ferne by the arm, but she shook him off. "You have no idea what it's like to starve, do you? Or freeze because you can't afford heating."

Penny moved next to Niall so she could see Ferne. "I'm sorry you're struggling, Ferne. You should have said something. We're your friends, we could have helped you." Daisy couldn't believe Penny was being so nice, even knowing Ferne was a killer.

Neither could Niall, who had now lost his famous Irish temper. "So, you thought you'd kill her? Is that how your convoluted mind works? And when you didn't succeed the first time, you followed her to the bus stop and tried again." He threw his hands in the air and turned to McGuinness. "She's insane. Arrest her."

"Like you would have helped me." Ferne laughed in Penny's face, her own mottled with anger. "Give me a break. All you're interested in is Sir-bloody-Barclay, here. Once you marry him, you'll never have to work again."

Niall froze.

Penny flushed. "That is not true. I love my job at the salon, and I wouldn't leave, no matter how much money I earned or who I married."

Daisy put an arm around her shoulder, pleased Penny had stood up for herself.

Ferne faced Niall. "Why do you think she's after you? You're old enough to be her father. Honestly, some men are so blind!"

Niall looked like he was about to throttle her. McGuinness put a warning hand on his chest.

"Buckley," he barked. "It's time to arrest Ferne for the murder of Melanie Haverstock and Ross Monroe, and the attempted murder of Penny Whitely."

Buckley stepped forward and began to read Ferne her rights, but she bolted towards Penny, her face twisted in rage. "I hate you! You have everything that I want, that I *deserve*, and you don't care. You don't even want it!"

Penny screamed as Ferne pummelled into her at full tilt. Daisy and Niall caught Penny to stop her from falling, while McGuinness grabbed Ferne. She twisted and bucked in his arms, but he held her in a vise-like grip. Spittle flew from her lips. "You deserve to die, you ungrateful bitch. I wish I'd killed you."

Chapter Twenty-four

After Ferne had been taken away by Buckley and the waiting police officers, the rest of the group collapsed into their chairs. Penny sat white-faced beside Niall, who didn't take his arm off her shoulder. Daisy hoped what Ferne had said hadn't spooked Niall. He was a renowned commitment-phobe. But that was a discussion for another day. Right now, they all needed a drink. She got out the two remaining bottles of prosecco that were in the refrigerator and poured everyone a glass. "I know we're not celebrating," she said, handing them out. "But I think we could all use a drink."

"Hear! Hear!" said Niall, downing his in one go. "That woman was barking mad."

Liz Roberts, who hadn't said a word the entire

evening, did the same. "I can't believe this had nothing to do with Melanie after all."

"She must have been harbouring that hatred towards Penny for years," said Floria, refilling her glass, then topping up Niall's. "Talk about screwed up."

Apple and Paloma sat in stunned silence clutching each other's hands. Their friend was a murderer.

"When did you work it out?" asked McGuinness, who'd refused a glass. He had to go back to the station and book Ferne.

Daisy sat next to him, cradling her champagne flute. "I figured it out last night when I got home from the pub. I was going through the sequence of events in my head, and I thought about how, at first, I assumed Ross had been killed because the attacker thought he was Krish, but they looked nothing alike—and then it struck me. Maybe Melanie was killed because she looked like someone else. Then it made sense. The lack of motive. The back alleyway. Nine o'clock. The pieces of the puzzle all fell together."

"Brilliant," said Krish, gazing at her with adoration. "You've got a knack for this sort of thing, Dais."

"Still working toward that criminology diploma?" asked Niall, who had dispensed with the glass and was drinking prosecco from the bottle.

She nodded.

"You'll be able to help the police in an official capacity soon." He winked at her.

McGuinness scowled at him.

Daisy felt bad for him. She'd stolen his thunder at the crucial moment, but there was no way he was going to work it out; he didn't have all the information.

"I didn't know she'd had a . . . What did you call it? A makeover?" he said sullenly.

"I tried to tell you," said Daisy. He hadn't wanted to know.

"Was she really a bottle-blonde?" asked Apple, who was recovering from the shock of her friend being named as the killer, now that she was nearing the end of her second glass of sparkling wine.

"That will teach me not to listen," muttered McGuinness.

"What about Ross?" asked Krish. "Why did she stab him outside the newsagent?"

"Ross decided to blackmail the suspects," Daisy explained. "That's what those threatening notes some of us got were about."

Liz looked down at her hands, while Yvette tilted her head up a notch.

"He sent them to every suspect in the investigation, and eventually he hit on the right person."

"Or the wrong one, depending on how you look at it," said Floria.

"I didn't get one," said Paloma, "but then, I haven't opened my mail since the wedding."

"I think you'll find you were sent one," said Daisy, then she looked at Apple. "You too, Apple."

Apple nodded. "I've been staying at my boyfriend's place, but I'll go home and look." She shivered. "I still can't believe Ferne killed two people. I've known her for years."

"Don't forget Penny," said Niall. "That's attempted murder."

McGuinness nodded. "Don't worry, we'll be charging her for that too."

Krish shook his head. "That's how I feel about Ross. I thought I knew the guy."

"There were several demand notices for unpaid council taxes on his desk," said Daisy. "I expect he needed the money and thought this was a clever way to get it."

"Stupid bastard," said Krish. "I wish he'd told me. Maybe I could have done something, prevented this from happening."

Liz drained her glass and stood up. "Well, that was an enlightening evening, Daisy, but I must go. Thank you for letting me in on your little denouement, Detective." McGuinness nodded as she walked past.

"Ferne did her a favour," piped up Asa from the back when Liz had left the salon. "Now she gets her husband back."

"Until next time," said Krish. At Daisy's stern look, he shrugged. "What? The guy's a billionaire dog-food magnate. He's bound to have women swarming over him. It's only a matter of time before he strays again."

Niall laughed. "Well, good luck to them." He turned to Penny. "Let's go home. I want to make sure you aren't after me just for my money."

Her eyes lit up. "Ferne had it all wrong."

He moved a lock of hair out of her face. "I know. The age difference does worry me, but I know how lucky I am to have you, so I'm going to selfishly hang on to you, and people can think what they like."

Daisy grinned. Any reservations she had about Niall had been put to rest.

Apple and Paloma were the next to leave. "I didn't realise she was so unhinged," Paloma said, still an unhealthy shade of pale. "And to think she was one of my bridesmaids."

"That was one crazy chick," Asa said, edging past McGuinness. "Daisy, I'm going to go now. I need to do something fun, like watch a comedy or go to a gig. This has been one intense evening."

"I know, thanks for staying, Asa." The young assistant left, dragging Bianca with her.

Krish came over. "I'm off, too, Daisy, but I wanted to give you this." He placed the key to Ross's apartment in her hand. "I don't need it anymore." She didn't meet his gaze, but handed the key over to McGuinness, who pocketed it without a word.

Floria and Yvette were talking quietly in the corner, or rather, Floria was the one talking, while Yvette listened with rapt attention.

"Well, it worked," Daisy said, giving McGuinness a bright smile. "She cracked and confessed, just like we hoped."

"Why didn't you tell me what you were thinking?" McGuinness studied her. "About Melanie being mistaken for Penny? Did you think I wouldn't listen? That I wouldn't believe you or something?"

His handsome face was tense, and Daisy could tell she'd hurt him by keeping it to herself. "It was late, and we'd been together the whole evening," she said, hoping he'd understand. "I thought it could wait until today, but then everybody arrived and I couldn't find the time to tell you. I'm sorry, I really did mean to."

He frowned. "Okay, I suppose that makes sense, but in the future, I'd like you to be honest with me from the get-go. About everything."

"I may not tell you everything straightaway," Daisy said, "but I'm always honest."

He took the key out of his pocket and studied it. "Not always."

Yikes. How had he known? They'd been so careful. Had somebody seen her climb out of the window at the apartment block? She bit her lip. "I don't know what you mean, Paul."

The corners of his mouth turned up. "You know exactly what I mean, Daisy, but I won't push it. Let's move on, shall we?"

"Oh, Floria!" Yvette cried, jumping to her feet. "*Merci. Ce magnifique!*"

Both Daisy and McGuinness turned around to find Yvette hugging Floria. Yvette never hugged anybody.

"What's going on?" Daisy asked with a smile, although she could guess.

"Floria has a friend who is a fashion designer and is prepared to invest in my boutique." Her cheeks were flushed with joy. "It means I won't have to close the store."

"That's wonderful," Daisy said. "What a great idea."

"Veronique will want her designs on display, of course," added Floria, her eyes sparkling, "but I'm sure you can come to some sort of arrangement."

"Of course," gushed Yvette, whom Daisy imagined was only too happy not to have to sell to Betting Direct. Now she could tell that Olaf where to shove it.

"I'm so happy. Thank you, Floria. You are a lifesaver."

"Veronique's solicitor will be in touch to iron out the details," said Floria.

Yvette couldn't stop thanking her. Eventually, in a haze of happiness, she waltzed out of the shop.

"That was a lovely thing you did." Daisy smiled at her friend.

"I must admit, I rely on Yvette's for last-minute supplies. I can't tell you how many times I've popped in there en route to the races to buy a pair of gloves or a hat. I couldn't have my favourite one-stop shop close down, now, could I?"

"No, indeed." Daisy squeezed her hand.

"Oh, did I tell you Mimi is coming to London the week after next?" Floria said, as she pulled on her coat. Mimi was Floria's half sister who lived in Australia. "She's doing a concert at the O2 Arena in December. I've got us all tickets." She grinned at DCI McGuinness. "That includes you, Inspector."

He grinned. "I'll look forward to it."

Daisy couldn't imagine the steely-eyed detective letting loose on the dance floor. That was something she'd pay good money to see.

"How long is Mimi here for?" she asked Floria.

"Indefinitely."

At Daisy's surprised look, she added, "Her agent wants her to build up her international following, starting in London. So she's here for at least six months, possibly longer. She's asked me to look into finding a property for her to rent in Edgemead."

"Why doesn't she stay at Brompton Court?" asked McGuinness. The manor house was huge, with something like eight bedrooms. Serena used to throw riotous weekend parties, and guests travelled from all over the country to stay in the majestic rooms. Daisy often thought that if Floria ever decided to sell, it would make a lovely hotel—except she knew that would never happen. Her friend was too emotionally tied to the place.

"Mimi says it gives her the creeps." Floria laughed, wrapping her scarf around her neck. "I can't say I blame her. I love the place, but I do shiver every time I walk over the spot where Mother died. As soon as I have time, I'm going to completely gut the place."

Daisy didn't want to know how much that would cost.

"But that's a project for another day," Floria continued. "Right now, I'm more than happy living in town with Josh and visiting Brompton Court on the weekends. It's an ideal arrangement. Josh plays rugby in Richmond every Saturday, so it's convenient for him too." Richmond was only a short distance from Edgemead. Daisy was so glad it had all worked out for Floria. It was great seeing her so happy.

She glanced at McGuinness, to find his eyes on her. She swallowed. Floria, as if sensing the change in mood, blew them a kiss and skipped out into the high street.

"Are you sure you won't have a glass?" Daisy asked him, for want of anything better to say. Her tongue seemed tied in knots all of a sudden.

He shook his head. "I can't, Daisy. I'm driving to Guildford now to talk to the prosecutor, after which I will be booking Ferne for the murders." He took a step closer to her. "I will, however, take a rain check on the prosecco."

Daisy felt her heart skip a beat. "You said that the last time."

He smiled at her, and for the first time all evening, his face softened and his grey eyes crinkled at the sides. "But this time, it's a promise. Unlike some people, I learn from my mistakes."

"Are you saying I don't?"

"Hmm . . ." He touched her cheek, then with a lingering smile, he walked out the door.

Don't miss the next delightful Daisy Thorne mystery by
Louise R. Innes

DEATH AT HOLLY LODGE

Coming soon from Kensington Publishing Corp.
Keep reading to enjoy a sample excerpt ...

Chapter One

"All I want for Christmas is you . . ." sang Daisy as she pulled into the gravel driveway outside Holly Lodge. Christmas was her favourite time of the year. Christmas trees glittered in windows, coffee shops served gingerbread lattes, and everybody was in a joyous mood.

She parked between Floria's racing-green MINI Cooper and a dirty, white van with a building company logo on the side. The sliding side door was open, displaying an assortment of tools, boxes, and a folded-up ladder. Renovations were in full swing.

She turned off the radio and climbed out of the car, her feet crunching on the frosty gravel. Holly Lodge was a Georgian-style family house that had once been rather grand, but had fallen into disrepair. She gazed up at the crumbling golden-brick exterior, admiring how it glowed in the weak, midmorning sun. The entrance was framed by rambling roses, which would be glorious in season, but were now a tangle of thorny twigs. Paint peeled off the front door, the porch looked worn and bare, and the windows were dirty and cracked. Only the holly bushes, after which the house had been named, seemed to thrive. Dark green and ripe with little red berries, they lined the drive and surrounded the front of the property.

Daisy took a deep breath, feeling the cold air infiltrate her lungs. It was stunning out here in the Surrey countryside. The rolling hills behind the lodge seemed to go on forever, until they disappeared into a hazy mist. Holly Lodge was situated between Edgemead, where Daisy lived, and the village of Cobham. Once a hunting lodge, it was only accessible by a single narrow lane, flanked on either side by a deep ditch, overgrown foliage, and then, endless meadows. In summer, they'd be filled with grazing cows and sheep from the nearby farm, but right now they were empty. Somewhere in the background, Daisy could hear a stream tinkling.

"Daisy, I'm so glad you could come!" Floria, her best friend, dashed out of the house and flung her arms around her. "Come inside, Mimi's dying to see you."

Daisy hugged her, then followed her inside and into a large entrance hall. "Wow." She gazed up at the high ceiling from which hung a grubby, but intricate chandelier. The walls were adorned with period features and elaborate cornices that would be lovely if they weren't covered with cobwebs.

"It needs a lot of work," said Floria. "But the design is classic and has heaps of potential."

The traditional flagstone flooring was chipped and cracked, and a team of contractors were pulling it up piece by piece and taking the tiles outside into the garden.

"Excuse the mess," called a lyrical voice from down the hall, and Mimi appeared. "They're gutting the interior before we can restore it."

"What a gorgeous place." Daisy smiled at Floria's half sister, who'd just arrived from Sydney. "I had no idea it was so spacious inside."

"Five bedrooms," Mimi told her. "But we're going to convert it into four, two with adjoining bathrooms." They embraced warmly. Daisy hadn't seen Mimi since her mother, the great opera diva Dame Serena Levanté, had passed away several years ago. Since then, Mimi had been busy making a name for herself in the music industry in her native Australia.

"How are you?" Daisy asked.

"I'm good." Mimi gave her a wide smile. She had a lovely heart-shaped face with the kind of flawless, glowing complexion that only celebrities seem to pull off. Her eyes were a striking green—identical to her late mother's—and she sported a crop of glossy black hair cut in a fashionable style. A tiny diamanté stud glittered in her nose. "A bit nervous about the upcoming European tour, but apart from that, everything's great."

"I'm sure they'll love you." Daisy gave her a reassuring smile. "Your latest single, 'That Night,' was a huge hit in the U.K. earlier this year. They didn't stop playing it on the radio." There was a rumour that Mimi had written it the night she'd met her husband, Rob.

Mimi grimaced. "I still feel like a small fish in a really big pond. Come on, let's sit in the kitchen, it's the only place that hasn't been dismantled yet. I'm afraid there's no heating. The boiler seems to be on the blink." She rolled her eyes. "Yet another thing that needs fixing."

"At least we can have a hot drink." Floria set about

making tea. "You shouldn't be nervous, Mimi. Didn't your manager say that the first gig at the O2 has already sold out?"

"That's great!" Daisy couldn't be happier for Mimi. She was so talented and from what Floria had told her, had worked extremely hard to get where she was. After her mother had died, leaving her and her sisters a substantial inheritance, she'd reinvented herself. She'd hired a voice coach, taken dance lessons, and hired a producer to record her demo tape. According to Floria, she'd put her heart and soul into her career, and amassed a legion of young fans in the process. After winning an Aria, one of Australia's most prestigious music awards, she was broadening her horizons and exploring the international pop market.

Mimi nodded. "Let's hope the rest of Europe sells as well."

"When is your first concert date?" Daisy took a seat at the rustic wooden table. The kitchen was in slightly better shape than the rest of the house, but the units were old and out of date, and bad linoleum had been laid over what Daisy suspected was a continuation of the period flagstone flooring. It was crying out for a makeover. "I'd love to come."

"The fifteenth of January," Mimi told her, accepting a cup of tea from Floria and straddling a chair opposite Daisy. "You must come. I'll get you all complimentary tickets."

"That would be amazing." Daisy grinned at Floria in excitement. "I can't wait."

Mimi ran a hand through her hair. "I've taken a month off to get settled, although these renovations are a pain.

I'm beginning to regret buying a house that requires so much work."

"Holly Lodge desperately needed someone to take care of it." Daisy glanced at the paint peeling off the walls. "It's been empty for so long, and it's such a beautiful old place. You've really done the house, and the village, a favour by taking it on."

"The grounds are lovely too," added Floria, sitting down. "The garden extends into the meadows and beyond that, into Hinchley Wood, and there's a stream behind the cottage with the cutest cobblestone bridge over it."

"That bridge is falling apart." Mimi widened her eyes in warning. "Don't use it until it's been repaired. The landscapers are coming next week, but trying to find people to work over the holidays is like wishing for a Christmas miracle. I'm having to pay them a fortune."

"It's a pity you didn't get this done before you arrived," said Daisy. "You're not living here while this is going on, are you?"

"Oh, gosh no. I'm staying at Brompton Court with Floria and Josh." She smiled at her sister. "They're putting me up."

"We've moved in for the holidays," added Floria, who had a townhouse in London's Chelsea District. She'd inherited Brompton Court, a grand country mansion, from her mother but she didn't live there. Instead, it was run by the capable Violeta and her husband, Pepe, the groundsman.

"Is Rob joining you for Christmas?" Daisy asked.

Mimi nodded. "Yeah, he's flying into Heathrow on Christmas Eve. Unfortunately, he has to stay and tie up some loose ends before he can knock off for the holidays." Mimi's husband, Rob Fallon, was the owner of the prestigious Fallon Hotel Group, which boasted a collection of upmarket boutique hotels in most of the world's capitals, London included. But like Mimi, his base was in Sydney, Australia.

"At least he'll be here for Christmas Day," Daisy said with a smile.

"So, what about you, Daisy?" asked Mimi, leaning forward over the back of the chair. Daisy noticed her nails were painted a shimmering green. "How are things at the salon?"

"Busy." She rolled her eyes. "It's a crazy time of year. We have back-to-back appointments, and the staff are run off their feet. The nail bar, a new addition for us, is doing extremely well, too."

"Well, it's nice of you to take time out to come and see me. We're all so grateful to you for solving Mother's murder. How is that handsome detective you were seeing?"

"Oh, I wasn't seeing him." The heat stole into Daisy's cheeks. "I was helping him."

"They're still not really seeing each other," said Floria, chuckling. "Even though Daisy's working with the police now in an informal capacity."

"Really? What are you doing?" Mimi asked.

"Oh, I'm just helping them with a bit of profiling. It's a part-time thing." She didn't like talking about it. In her experience, people tended to clam up when you mentioned you worked for the police, so only her closest friends knew.

"Impressive." Mimi arched an eyebrow. "So, tell me, why haven't you got together with that hunky detective yet?"

A loud crash in the living room made them jump.

Daisy breathed a sigh of relief. *She* didn't know what her relationship with Detective Chief Inspector McGuinness was, so how could she explain it to anyone else?

"What was that?" Mimi leaped off her chair.

Daisy and Floria followed her into the lounge, where two red-faced contractors stood gazing at a sooty fireplace that was big enough to park a car in.

"What happened?" Mimi waved her hand in front of her face. A fine black mist hung in the air, and a heap of blackened debris had fallen out of the chimney.

"The chimney is blocked," one of the men told her. "Someone has wedged several wooden slats up it. We're trying to unblock it now."

"Wooden slats?" Floria frowned. "Why would they do that?"

"Maybe they didn't use it and wanted to shut off the draft?" Daisy suggested. These mammoth chimneys were often drafty. The one in her little cottage, which was a fraction of the size of Holly Lodge, had been the same until she had wood-burning ovens installed.

"Could be," agreed the other contractor. "We'll get it cleared and working properly, don't you worry."

"It'll look lovely once it's done," said Floria. "A real focal point."

"Why don't you show me the rest of the property?" Daisy gazed eagerly out of the windows at the expanse of garden and in the distance, the hazy meadows and the shadowy, purple woods. "I haven't been here since I was a kid. Back then it was owned by the Lyle family."

"They went bankrupt, apparently," said Mimi. "The real estate agent told me it's been empty since old Mr. Lyle passed away five years ago."

"So sad . . ." Daisy murmured. She had fond memories of picnicking in the meadows with her friends when she was a teenager, and later walking through the woods with Tim. She blinked. Now where had that come from? She hadn't thought about her ex-boyfriend in ages. Shaking her head, she followed Mimi and Floria outside, through patio doors that were so cracked and dirty it was impossible to see through them.

"These will have to be replaced," remarked Floria, echoing Daisy's thoughts.

"My interior designer, Tamara, is working with the building contractors. She did the Rochester, Rob's hotel in Mayfair, so I'm trusting her with Holly Lodge. She's got a wonderful eye for detail."

"I catered a fiftieth at the Rochester last month." Floria's company, Prima Donna Productions, organised events and parties for the rich and famous. "It's stunning. Tamara knows her stuff. You're in good hands."

"Wow, I can see how the lodge got its name. There's holly everywhere." Daisy ran her fingers over the distinctive jagged leaves on an oversized bush bursting with red berries outside the patio door. "It looks so Christmassy."

"Some of it will have to be cut back." Mimi stood in the middle of the garden and inspected the house. "It seems to have taken over."

From this angle, Daisy could see the window frames were cracked and peeling and many of the tiles on the roof were missing. It was a big job—expensive too. No wonder it had remained unoccupied for so long.

A gurgling stream ran through the bottom of the garden, and she could see that Floria was right: The curved cobblestone bridge looked like something out of a fairy tale. She could almost imagine a big, ugly troll hiding underneath amongst the bulrushes. "Once the garden is done, you can sit out here and listen to the babbling brook while you compose your songs," she mused.

Mimi smiled. "That's the idea. As soon as I saw the stream, I fell in love with the place. And the view stretches for miles over the meadows and into the woods. It's idyllic, and so different from my place in Sydney."

"But your property over there is stunning," said Floria, who'd been over to visit. "It's so modern and spacious, and you have a breathtaking view of the harbour bridge."

"Yes, but it's not green and lush like this." Mimi ran her hand along the top of the low stone wall that separated the stream from the garden and took a deep breath. "I love the smell of fresh country air."

"That's probably manure from the neighbouring paddock," Floria pointed out.

Daisy laughed.

A guttural yell made them glance back at the house.

"I hope those guys aren't destroying that fireplace," muttered Mimi. "Tamara wants to preserve as many of the original features as possible."

"We'd better go and see." Floria set off up the garden path towards the lodge.

"I think you'll be very happy here," Daisy told Mimi as they followed her.

"I hope so. This will be our London base, so to speak, so we want to make it as homey as possible."

An eerie silence greeted them as they stepped through the open patio door into the living room. The two burly men were staring at the fireplace, their faces pale beneath the soot. A handful of other contractors had accumulated around them. All eyes were focused on the chimney.

"Is there a problem?" Mimi asked, then Floria gasped and grabbed her arm.

"Mimi, look!"

Daisy took a step closer, and her heart jumped into her throat. "Is–Is that a body?"

Through the black dust, she saw the figure of a man lying in a crumpled heap on the charred bricks. He was surrounded by broken boards and covered in dirt and grime.

"He toppled out of the chimney when we took out the last of the boards," said one of the contractors. "Goodness knows how long he's been up there."

"Oh Lord." Mimi's hand flew to her mouth.

Daisy bent down to have a closer look.

"Careful, Daisy," urged Floria, who was still clutching her sister's arm.

Daisy waved away the dust and stared down at the unfortunate man. His skin was sallow and tight across his face, like parchment stretched to its breaking point. His vacuous eyes were sunken into his head, exposing most of the sockets. Thin strands of grey hair protruded from his leathery scalp like a zombie version of Einstein. It was then that she saw the dark, gaping wound at the side of his head covered in congealed blood. She studied it for some time, before her eyes were drawn away by his beard. Despite the thinning hair and obvious decomposition, he had a full, white fluffy beard. It couldn't possibly be real. Then she noticed what he was wearing, and her eyes widened.

"Who is it?" whispered Floria. "Do we know him?"

"I'm afraid so." Daisy turned to face them. "It's Father Christmas—and he's been murdered."